THE CAPE MAY MURDERS

A Mystery Novella

CHRISTOPHER MICHAEL BLAKE

Published by Christopher Michael Blake, LLC

Lanoka Harbor, New Jersey

www.Christophermichaelblake.com

October 25, 2022
Wednesday 2:00am

"Chasing tumble weeds." That was the phrase Officer William Preston, Billy to his co-workers, used to describe working the overnight shift in Cape May during the late fall and winter months. Although it still was technically the fall, without the sun and the whipping winds from all sides of the ocean and adjacent canal, the cold nights already felt close enough to winter. Sitting in his squad car just after two on this late cold October night, the temperature outside was already below freezing. Gusts of wind blew against the windows shaking his patrol vehicle just a tad.

Billy could see his breath hanging in the cold air outside the car. But, inside the marked police vehicle with the engine running and the heat on, Billy had no problems staying warm. Feeling as if he was overheating and removed his oversized black North

Face jacket. Settling into his night shift, Billy Preston reached into his bag to remove the wrapped Ham and Swiss with mayo and lettuce sub sandwich he purchased from the West Side market off Broad Street. The west side market was one of the few remaining independent restaurants left in the area; shopping there allowed Billy to reminisce about a time in Cape May where there were no Subway or Wawa chain stores, just mom-and-pop restaurants.

Parking the patrol car on Fisherman's Wharf just after the bridge coming off the parkway south into Cape May on the last exit of the New Jersey Parkway, Officer Preston unwrapped the packaging of his Ham and Swiss and took the first bite of his nighttime lunch meal. Technically, Preston was looking for speeders coming over the bridge as he sat in the parking lot chewing with his mouth full. His vehicle was idling between the white building with black lettering reading Tony's Marine Railway to his right and the yellow-green letter sign which read The Lobster House to his left. The front fender of the police car was pulled back from the road just a tad so as not to give his position away to any oncoming speeders.

Across the street from Preston, the aisle of seafood and independent pizza restaurants mixed with antique shops was his only view in the windy quiet. Briefly distracted as he opened the bag of UTZ potato chips and glanced away, he pulled the bag apart and heard the crisp sound of freshness in the pop of the bag before stopping in mid-ergonomic motion. A mid-aged blonde woman in a white dressing gown and brown sandals was walking in the middle of the street, using the double yellow line for direction heading into town. Her hands were open on her side as if cupped in mid-air, and the golden locks of blonde air flowed and moved with the oncoming funnels of wind. The white sheer gown blew tight against her bosom as she walked into the wind.

Preston had to snap himself out of what he was witnessing. His first instinct was that he must be imagining things as the woman walked at a slow pace down route six-thirty-three. Then he thought the woman must be a ghost. This must be what looking at a spirit, a pale phantom, or a specter looks like. The wind whipped through her hair and dress, and despite the bitter cold air outside the woman moved with non-descriptive movements, keeping a slow steady pace. The woman's white clouds of breath proved she was alive. Even thirty feet from where Preston was sitting, he could see the cold white oxygen she breathed rise from her mouth and disappear into the dark.

Putting on the headlights and overhead flashers and placing the car into gear, Preston rolled ahead of the thin, white-gowned woman who did not seem alarmed at the flashing lights or concerned with his presence. Exiting the vehicle, Preston forgot to put his North Face winter coat back on and was struck by the immediate chill of the night as he closed his car door and approached the woman.

"Ma'am? Ma'am? Are you alright? Can I help you?" Officer Preston asked, removing his flashlight from his holster, and shining the light into her eyes.

Shining the flashlight in her eyes seemed to have awoken the woman from her daze as she stared at him and then, realizing she was cold, wrapped her arms around her bosom.

"I am so cold." The woman mumbled, repeating the words over and over as they grew into a whisper.

"Who are you, and where are you heading?"

"I am so cold." The woman repeated as Preston noticed her lips had grown blue and her face a bright red color in the cheeks as her forehead appeared to flush.

"Let's get you inside the back of my vehicle, and I can take your information from there." Preston encouraged her, escorting the woman to the back of his vehicle and opening the back door as the woman in white sat down.

Preston reached for his car door and climbed back behind the wheel. The back seat where the woman passenger sat was divided by a screen enmeshed in plexiglass with small round pockets to speak through. Preston turned around in the cab of the squad car and started the conversation over.

"Miss, could you please tell me where you were going tonight?"

"I don't know. I can't remember."

"Can you tell me your name or address?"

"I...I can't remember."

"Is there anything you do remember?"

"Only the cold." The woman responded. Picking up the radio transmitter, Preston held the mic down.

"Preston to dispatch, come in dispatch."

"Go ahead, Billy," Lorraine huffed from the Cape May Police Department.

"Lorraine, I have a scantily dressed woman with amnesia walking over the bridge down six-thirty-three into town," Preston radioed.

"Sounds like your night is going better than mine. Do you need emergency services to respond?" Lorraine asked.

"No, aside from some amnesia, she seems okay. I don't see sense in waking EMS to come out here, and I don't have much going on here. I will drive her to the Cape May Regional Medical Center."

"Copy. Don't stay out too late." Lorraine ribbed him.

"Yes, mom," Preston replied, placing the radio microphone back into its holder on the dashboard panel and placing the car into gear. Looking into the rearview mirror at his passenger, he could see a blank aimless stare as the amnesic woman glared out the window over the bridge and onto the canal.

* * *

Off the southern tip of Cape May, about twenty miles from shore, the thirty-foot boat the Mail Order Bride had halted its throttle. The ship's driver silenced the motor and looked back at the beach from the top deck to see the beam of light emanating from the still active beacon atop the Cape May lighthouse toward the sea, spinning round in circles. The coast guard still used the lighthouse built in eighteen fifty-nine with the beacon light extending twenty-four miles out to sea. It was the third lighthouse built on Cape May, with the other two lighthouses lost to erosion.

The driver of the boat grabbed the plastic hooded mask and placed it over his head before heading down the ladder to the deck and approaching the wooden chest. Dressed in a black cloak, the boat driver was now in full costume, wearing a mask of skull and bone, and the hooded black cloak representative of the Grim Reaper.

The Reaper removed a key from under their cloak pocket and placed it into the chest, unlocking the padlock on the latch. The click of the lock sound was lost as the ocean waves lapped onto the side of the boat and retreated away, rocking the ship slightly to and fro. The Reaper lifted the top of the chest and stared at the man bound inside. The elderly man was bound with sixty pounds of steel chain secured with no less than fifteen different padlocks.

The victim inside the trunk lifted his eyes at the Reaper, catching the plastic face mask in the light of the rotating light emanating from the lighthouse. The bound man still appeared foggy from the drugs, but something in his eyes gave the slightest bit of lucid recognition of what was occurring. Reaching into the Reaper's cloak pocket, the Reaper produced a syringe, and removing the plastic cap, the Reaper reached down and plunged the tip of the needle into the bound victim's neck.

Taking care not to put too much of the Devil's Breath into his victim's neck, the Reaper withdrew the syringe. The Reaper was surprised by the power of the Devil's Breath, also known as Scopolamine, having heard of its ability to render victims docile and incapable of exercising free will. The Devil's Breath originated in Bogota, Colombia, from the Borrachero tree. Once extracted, the Scopolamine exhibits odorless, colorless, and tasteless, often producing strange dreams in its victims.

As the bound man in the trunk nodded their head down and closed his eyes to sleep, the Reaper wondered if the man was dreaming now. Was he dreaming of the Reaper? Did he see the Reaper's face in his dream? Had he the slightest clue about what was about to happen? The Reaper tossed the syringe out to sea and began unlocking the chains binding him before closing the trunk lid and relocking the padlock on the front latch.

Bending forward, the Reaper began to push the trunk toward the front of the boat. The deck was slippery from the mist of the crashing waves combined with the weight of the man inside the chest and the additional sixty pounds of steel chain. Moving the trunk across the stern was difficult, as the Reaper experienced problems obtaining solid footing.

After an exhausting effort, the trunk went off the side of the boat, with the Reaper almost losing balance and having their momentum carry them off the side of the Mail Order Bride. Standing up and stretching, the Reaper could see the trunk bob and weave as it floated in the Atlantic. A small hole no bigger than the tip of a pencil had been drilled into the bottom of the trunk, ensuring a slow drowning death of the sleeping man inside.

Removing their face mask and cloak, the Reaper regained their position at the helm on the top deck of the Mail Order Bride. Taking the boat across the Atlantic away from Cape May Point and north towards the canal where the Reaper had appropriated the Mail Order Bride for the night from Utsch's Marina on the canal's east end. Careful to remove all traces of the crime or the boat being used for the evening, the Mail Order Bride was returned to its slip spot, retied to the ballast, and wiped clean with no evidence of the boat's role in the death of Gilbert Epson.

October 25, 2022
Wednesday 9:15am

Pulling his government issued Ford Police Interceptor into his reserve parking spot in front of the Cape May Police Department Municipal building, Clyde Browning pulled the visor down over the steering wheel and stared at himself in the mirror. Chief of Police Browning removed a black plastic comb from his front pocket and threaded the black needle points of the comb through his thick hair, being careful not to have one hair misplaced as he pulled his colored hair back.

Not too bad looking a fellow, he thought. He may be the best sixty-year-old in New Jersey.

Browning's hair was artificially dyed black, but the coloring was not overly evident in his mind. His gut didn't protrude over his belt yet and running three miles down the concrete boardwalk of Cape May on the beach after work four times a week also assisted in keeping his health in check. Staring at his pale blue eyes in the mirror, Browning began nodding at himself.

"Thirty more days. After Thanksgiving, it's on to Key West permanently." Browning said to himself out loud. He was a little surprised he was thinking of his pending retirement. A lifestyle change on the horizon filled with sun, booze, and marlin fishing. Giving up all he had known and worked for over the past thirty-five years. His pension and house sale would cover years of expenses even in an area as affluent as Key West.

Shutting the visor, Browning opened the car door and felt a gust of wind from the previous evening still flowing through the air messing with the masterpiece of hair design he had spent the last few minutes creating in the car. Pulling his cap on his head, Browning pushed forward over to the sidewalk and the brown brick municipal building and, using an excessive amount of force, pulled open the glass door against the wind. The glass door slammed shut behind him as he stepped through the vestibule of the Police department.

Browning was met with greetings and smiles from the few officers, dispatchers, and detectives already at work this morning. The Cape May Police Department consisted of twenty-two officers, four communication officers, and one civilian administrative assistant. The most considerable expenditure was the summertime hiring of twenty seasonal officers to assist with the more than small four-point three square miles of Cape May jurisdiction. An increase in residents from just over five thousand to over ten thousand was not uncommon for the summer months, in addition to the number of visitors numbering the hundreds of thousands.

But in late October, the seasonal officers were already gone, as were the extra vacationers or shoebie's as the residents at the New Jersey shore still called their guests. The term shoebie was an early nineteen-twenties expression used to describe day trippers from Philadelphia or New York to the Jersey shore who often brought their lunch with them in their shoe box.

Before entering his office, Clyde stopped mid-gait before turning and approaching the desk of his secretary Carrie Stewart. Stewart had been the secretary for his predecessor in the department and, with any luck, would outlast the incoming Chief of Police as well.

"Anything going on?" Browning asked as he picked up the mail and began rifling through the inscriptions of the incoming letters and brown manila envelopes of departmental correspondence.

Covering the handheld telephone line receiver with her hand, "The new Chief of Police is in your office. He's been waiting for about a half hour." Carrie whispered.

"He's here earlier than I thought he would be," Browning answered, placing the mail under his right armpit.

"I brought him some coffee, black, no sugar. Also, do you need me to tell you about what happened to Billy last night while on patrol? "

"What did the idiot do now? He didn't shoot anyone did he?"

"Finally, a piece of information you don't have. A near-naked woman with amnesia appeared from over the Cape May Bridge. She had nearly frozen to death. Billy transported her to Cape Regional Medical Center. Last I heard, she was still there under observation." Carrie gossiped, still covering the phone with her wrinkled right hand and wrist of fake pearls dangling from the loose skin.

"Thanks, Carrie."

"Do you want me to assign a detective to interview her?" She asked.

"No. I think I'll go out there and talk to the amnesic woman myself. Maybe I'll take the new Chief with me and get to know him."

"She's a pretty girl, from what I understand." Carrie winked her right eye, reading what was on the Chief's mind.

Closing the door behind him as he entered his office, the new Chief of Police sat with his back to the door facing the front of the cherry oak desk. Pictures and certificates of achievement lined the faded white walls of the office, which hadn't been painted in the last fifteen years. Browning entered the office, the man who would replace him turned his head upon hearing the door shut behind him and rose to his feet, turning and extending out his right hand.

"Chief Browning, I'm John McNamara. I'll be taking over for you at the end of next month." McNamara said, shaking Browning's hand. His grip was firm, and he was well dressed in navy blue pants with a white shirt. The nameplate on his breast pocket embroidered in gold with black lettering read Chief John J. McNamara.

"You are younger than I thought you'd be. I pictured someone short with grey, white hair in their mid-fifties taking my place." Browning said sternly, moving past the still-standing McNamara to the opposite side of the cherry-stained wood desk, placing the departmental mail on top of the keyboard.

"If you doubt my expertise, you could raise the issue with the town council who hired me," McNamara replied.

"No. That won't be necessary. I wasn't much older than you when I took over as Chief of Police here twenty years ago. Besides, it's the town's choice, not mine. So, tell me, why are you here a month early? Halloween is at the end of the week, and I don't retire until after Thanksgiving. "

"I left my last duty assignment early, packed up, and came out here. It's been my experience that a new supervisor learns best from watching what his predecessor did and not implementing any change immediately. People tend to hold things back when a new supervisor comes on board. Thirty days here, I should be ready to jump right in without missing a beat instead of playing catch-up with you gone." McNamara explained.

"Well, I would offer you some tea or coffee, Ms. Stewart, the secretary makes an excellent cup of Joe, but I have other obligations to attend to this morning," Browning added.

"I already have a cup, thanks."

"Last night there was an amnesic woman who was found out by the Cape May Bridge by one of our officers, she was damn near naked from what I understand. I'm heading over to the Cape May Regional Medical Center by the Courthouse to see if she remembers anything. Maybe she'll let me do a fingerprint check and DNA swab if necessary." Browning said.

"Is it always standard protocol for the Chief to go on routine assignments and conduct fingerprint and DNA checks on amnesic patients?" McNamara asked.

"It's the golden rule. He who wears the crown makes the rules. For the next thirty days, I am still wearing the crown, so it's still my rules. If you want, you can stay here and answer the phone about the upcoming Halloween pageant held this weekend when it rings every half hour. Calls should start coming in about another fifteen minutes. But personally, I hear the dame they brought in last night was a knock-out, and I'd much rather talk to her than the shop owners on the other end of the phone."

"I thought the golden rule applied to gold, not crowns," McNamara inquired.

"Today, it applies to whatever the hell I say it should." Browning retorted.

"Then I guess I should go and get the ink pad, fingerprint card, and DNA swab set," McNamara answered.

"I thought you might see things my way," Browning said with a grin as he sat down and opened his mail from that morning.

* * *

The two men traveled north on the Parkway. The Cape May Court House was attached to the Cape May Regional Hospital just under twelve miles from the shore town, past Stone Harbor but before the Cape May County Zoo. Where southern Cape May hosted antique shops, restaurants, bars, and two-bedroom, one-bath bungalows, just over the bridge was a desolate parkway with wildlife management reservations and woods mixed with wetlands before branching out to the shore towns of Ocean City and Avalon.

Browning drove while McNamara remained silent, taking the scenery from the passenger seat. The silence between the two men filled the vacuum of the ten-minute drive to the hospital without a word passing between them. Browning wondered what McNamara was thinking as he looked at the oncoming traffic in the opposite lane and the windowed shops with their large business banners and American flags blowing in the late October wind.

Arriving at the hospital lifted an unbearable weight to open his mouth and speak to his replacement. To be able to talk to the man like a person, not like his replacement. When the two men got out of the Interceptor, McNamara finally spoke.

"Are you going to miss it?"

"Miss what?" Browning asked, the two police officers walking side by side through the parking lot to the front vestibule of the hospital.

"Work. Cape May. The people. Any of it?" McNamara asked as the two uniformed officers checked in with security at the front desk and received a room number for their Jane Doe.

"Sometimes I worry I might. You'll find most of your time is spent dealing with the storefront owner's constant complaints about small mundane items during the business of the summer months. The town council will constantly badger you about overtime expenditures and coverage for every holiday event. Those are the reasons why I won't miss this job." Browning said, taking a breath as the two men got on the nearest elevator.

"So, what are the reasons you will miss this place?" McNamara asked.

"Only one. It's my unshakeable belief that Cape May will fall apart without me being here. Silly and unrealistic, I know. The town will continue on day in and day out, no matter who is in charge. But, because Cape May will go on without me, I have my doubts about whether I have done any good serving here in the last thirty years. To be so easily replaced shows how insignificant I really am. You must think that's naïve of me." Browning explained as the elevator opened.

"No, I think your reflections have a poetic awareness to them," McNamara conceded.

"Don't get all artsy on me now, son," Browning said with a smile. "Follow my lead here. We'll get her to consent to do the fingerprints and

DNA swabs but try not to say anything unnecessary. She's been through enough." Browning instructed as McNamara nodded in ascent, and the two men entered Jane Doe's room.

* * *

Browning entered the room of Jane Doe and was slightly taken aback. The blonde amnesic woman was prettier than he imagined she would be. She was in her early to mid-thirties, sitting upright in the bed and being spoken to by a doctor asking her to follow his pen light with her eyes back and forth. The woman and the doctor looked at the visitors entering the room before resuming the eye test. Browning and McNamara crowded the doorway as the doctor turned his pen light off and began scribbling on his clipboard. Browning tried to look over the shoulder of the Doctor whose nameplate read B. Stannis to see what he was writing but couldn't read the sloppy handwriting.

"Now, I am going to ask you some basic questions. Don't think too hard about the answers. Just respond with the first thought you have, alright?" Dr. Stannis instructed.

"Ok." Jane Doe nodded.

"What year is it?"

"2022"

"Where are you at currently?"

"The hospital." She replied.

"What state are you in?"

"New Jersey." She smiled, answering without missing a beat.

"Where do you live?"

"I don't remember."

"What is your name?"

"I don't know."

"What is your mother's first name?"

"I don't remember."

"What was your favorite television show growing up?"

"Bugs Bunny," Jane giggled with a smile.

"Thank you. I think you are going to be just fine. These gentlemen behind me are Police Officers. Maybe they can help fill in some of the blanks." Dr. Stannis said.

"Doctor, will my memory return?" Jane Doe asked.

"Oh yes, I think it definitely will." Dr. Stannis said before wedging past McNamara and Browning to leave the room.

"Ma'am. My name is Chief Clyde Browning, and this is Chief John McNamara. We understand you had a rough night, but we need to know if you have any loved ones who need to be contacted. A husband, brothers, father, mother, friends?"

"I don't know. Maybe." Jane Doe answered with her bright brown eyes looking at both men.

"It's fine. There may be a way to help you. With your permission, Chief McNamara would like to fingerprint you and run a swab with his Q-tip on the inner part of your cheek for DNA. It's possible we might identify you through our national registration system or national DNA database. Would that be acceptable?"

The blonde woman sitting on the bed nodded her consent, and Browning nodded to McNamara, who placed plastic gloves on his hands before approaching the bed.

"If you could, relax your fingers and allow me to press them onto the white index card one at a time." McNamara placed one finger at a time, rolling the inked fingers onto the card, careful not to smudge them. Then taking all five fingers together and move them in ink before pressing them together on the card. With the fingerprints completed, McNamara handed the index card to Browning.

When McNamara produced the Q-tip vial, Jane Doe took a Kleenex tissue to her fingers to remove the ink from her hands.

"This is a DNA swab. It won't hurt, but I will ask you to open your mouth as I lightly brush the inside of your cheek for a sample and put it back in the vial. Is that alright with you?"

"Yes." Jane Doe said, opening her mouth as McNamara removed the Q-tip and swabbed the inside of the cheek for saliva, replacing the Q-tip back into the vial.

"There. All done." McNamara said, smiling. "So, how long will it take for you to find out if there's a match in the system for me?" Jane Doe asked.

McNamara looked to Browning, who nodded.

"If I can get the samples to the State Police this afternoon, it may take a day or two on the fingerprints. If we rely on DNA, and it's not in the State database, they will refer it to the National Database, which could take a few more days."

"A few days?" Jane Doe asked.

"No longer than a few days at best," McNamara answered.

"Can't we just take my picture and place it on the internet or the news asking people to come forward if they know who I am?"

"That's never a good idea," Browning interjected. "There have been issues in the past with men who arrive at the hospital with a fake story claiming to know a female, which later turns out to be false. We would rather be certain to send you home with your family."

"I understand."

"Please be patient. We'll find out who you are soon enough. Just take it easy and relax." Browning said with a smile before both men turned and left as McNamara followed Browning out of the room.

Browning and McNamara stood waiting in the hallway for the elevator when Dr. Stannis, who was examining their Jane Doe, walked past them, and Browning stopped him.

"Excuse me, Doctor, can I have a minute of your time?" Browning asked.

"What can I do for you, gentlemen?" Doctor Stannis answered.

"What can you tell us about the onset of Jane Doe's amnesia?" Browning asked.

"What do you mean?"

"I mean, what could have caused it? Was it a bump on the head?"

"Oh, of course...there is nothing physically wrong with that young woman in there. No bumps on the head, scans all returned negative, cognition and reflexes are excellent."

"So, she's faking?" Browning asked.

"Not necessarily. I believe there may have been a mental break, an underlying psychological episode which caused that young woman's memory to shatter."

"I am not following you, Doctor Stannis."

"Look, I am not a psychologist, so it is only my opinion, but when I asked her general questions, where are you? What year is it? What was your favorite cartoon growing up? She was able to answer those questions with no problems. But if you ask a personal question about her identity, she draws a blank. It leads me to believe she may have suffered a psychological trauma which led to the amnesia she suffers from."

"What would you recommend?" Browning asked.

"I have the number of a good psychologist, a friend of mine. Dr. McDonough, I would recommend she see him for a consult. Maybe talking about the issues will bring back some of the memories."

"Thanks, Doctor. I'll call you later for that reference. This is our elevator." Browning said as the elevator dinged open.

October 25, 2022
Wednesday 11:45am

"Biaggi's has the best barbeque pulled pork in Cape May and all of South Jersey," Browning boasted, opening the door to the pizzeria and deli. Biaggi's sat on the corner of Beach Ave and Perry Street, across from the Cape May promenade. The promenade was a paved concrete stretch path parallel to the beach and the Atlantic Ocean and across from the Beach Avenue shops.

The township of Cape May decided to move from a wooden boardwalk to a paved concrete promenade after the Nineteen Sixty-two Nor'easter destroyed the previous wooden boardwalk. During the Nor'easter of Nineteen sixty-two, the entirety of Beach Ave was erased along with the previous Convention Hall and over twelve hundred dwellings.

All of the earlier shops and hotels lining the three-mile stretch of the boardwalk were lost to the sea.

Biaggi's shop was empty except for the older thin gentlemen behind the counter with a thick mustache and bald head wearing a horseshoe of hair from ear to ear. An older obese woman with larger hands waved at the men as they entered the pizzeria. Browning returned the pair's greetings with a wave of his own, indicating an air of familiarity exchanged amongst friends.

"Chief McNamara, I want to introduce you to Antonio and Patricia Biaggi," Browning said.

"How are you both doing?" McNamara said greeting the pair and exchanging pleasantries with the elderly shop owners.

"So, this is your replacement. If you ask me, you should stay on as Chief and not let that council force your hand at retirement." Antonio Biaggi chided while wiping his hands off on a dish towel.

"I've told you, Tony, I made this decision about retirement on my own. No one is forcing me to retire, and I am very much looking forward to fishing marlin all day in Key West at the end of next month," Browning chirped.

"If you say so, Clyde. The residents of Cape May will never understand what you mean to them until you are gone." Antonio Biaggi responded.

"I assure you, I am leaving the beautiful Cape May to the entrusted and well-able hands of my replacement Chief McNamara," Browning replied.

"Tony, don't badger the man and be rude in front of our new Chief of Police. What will it be today, gentlemen?" Patricia Biaggi asked.

"We'll each have an order of your Barbeque pulled pork sandwiches with Pepsi's," Browning ordered without consulting McNamara about his order preference.

"Have a seat. I'll bring it right out." Patricia smiled as Antonio went back to needling the dough on the counter.

Taking a seat at a table just out of earshot of the Biaggi's, Browning leaned close to McNamara and whispered, "Don't let the old man fool you; he's got a good reason to be concerned about what happens in Cape May. He owns this entire block of stores on Beach Avenue; the man is a multi-millionaire. The renters of these adjacent shops all pay a high amount of rent to him each month. When an event like this week's Halloween parade occurs, you can bet the first telephone call you'll receive is from Mr. Biaggi. He sat on the town council with me for a long time, from the early nineties until about ten years ago. It may well have been his influence that ended up making me Chief."

"Why isn't he on the town council now if he wants to have a say on what goes on?" McNamara asked.

"It's a long story, but to sum up, the residents of Cape May at first enjoyed having five township members vote and input their suggestions. But as time goes on, more and more people got left out of the decision-making process, and more and more residents' policies don't get implemented. Taxes go up, specific individuals receive perceived preferential treatment, and there is backlash. Time builds enemies.

"The longer a group is in power, the more enemies they make. One by one, we were all eventually voted off the council and replaced. Soon Biaggi didn't have the votes or power to implement what his constituents wanted, his friends disappeared, and he was replaced. Here comes our food." Browning said, turning to Patricia Biaggi carrying two plates of Barbeque pulled pork on submarine rolls, each with a bag of potato chips.

"I'll be right back with your drinks," Patricia said, turning back to the counter and reaching for the plastic cups.

"Dig in. The food is excellent. Just be careful to avoid getting any of the juice splatter on your clean shirt." Browning quipped.

As Browning took the first large bite of his barbeque pulled pork sandwich, Mrs. Biaggi returned and placed the drinks on the table and straws on top of the cups. McNamara got the impression from the look on the woman's face as if she wanted to say something to Browning, but before opening her mouth, Browning's cell phone rang interrupting her thoughts.

Browning wiped his hands on the napkins from the dispenser and placing his bi-focal reading glasses on his face to read the caller identification on the cell phone. Reading the caller's name, Browning clicked the red answer button and held the cell phone to his ear. The dismissive action put any chance of Patricia Biaggi speaking with Browning on hold, and she turned away, heading back to behind the counter, and fell out of earshot next to her husband.

"I understand. Tell her I'll come right over. I should be there in about a half hour. Right. Okay, thanks, Carrie." Browning said, turning the cell phone off and replacing it in his top right breast pocket.

"That was our secretary Ms. Stewart. She received a call from Danielle Epson. It appears her husband, Gil, never came home last night." Browning said, taking another bite of his sandwich while the barbeque sauce poured out the bottom of the submarine roll.

"Don't we have detectives who follow up on missing persons?" McNamara asked.

"We do, but this is personal. Gilbert Epson served on the town council with Biaggi and me. We were always amicable towards one another, but we had a falling out after the town council voted us out. His wife would consider it important to have me notified via phone and be personally involved." Browning said, filling his mouth with another bite of sandwich.

"Is this something we should be concerned about? You know, out of character for Mr. Epson?" McNamara asked.

"Disappearing is definitely not in Gilbert Epson's character. The poor old fuddy-duddy would have to get his wife's permission just to break wind. Not coming home is definitely something to be concerned about." Browning said, taking the remaining bit of roll and running it through the spilled barbeque sauce on the plate before placing the soggy roll in his mouth.

"Then, shouldn't we leave and go and interview Mrs. Epson?" McNamara suggested.

"If he's been missing since yesterday, then fifteen more minutes won't matter to anyone except for me missing my lunch. Besides, you are not going." Browning answered, taking a slurp of his Pepsi.

"I will drop you off back at the station, get a car from Carrie and drop off Jane Doe's fingerprints and DNA at the State Police. I'll handle the interview with Mrs. Epson." Browning said, opening the bag of potato chips.

While Browning plunged fingerfuls of potato chip after potato chip into his mouth, McNamara took slow, deliberate bites of his sandwich as if he had lost his appetite.

"What's wrong, not impressed with barbeque sauce?" Browning asked with a gluttonous mouthful of sandwich.

"No, the food's fine. I was just curious, what is the worst case you ever worked on during your time here in Cape May?" McNamara asked.

"The worst case I ever worked on?" Browning reflected, taking another sip of Pepsi. "Back when I was a patrolman in the early nineties, this is before I became Chief understand. I had only been on the force for a few years when the entire county of Cape May was put on alert about a missing girl. Jennifer Martin, I can remember her name like yesterday. I knew the child briefly, running into her mainly through her mom Linda. The mother was a real beauty, with a husband who worked in an office all day and was never home.

"Anyway, one day, the nine-year-old girl, Jennifer, goes missing. Disappears, and no one sees anything. I mean, poof, the girl's gone. Checkpoints are set up on the outgoing lanes of Lafayette and Delaware streets. The outbound lane to the Cape May bridge is shut down. House-to-house searches are conducted, volunteers scour the beach, and hotlines looking for information are set up. We did everything we could. For a week, the investigation continues, and we know deep down every day Jennifer is gone, the chances of getting her back alive are slim.

"Then, in an instant, everything changes. An anonymous tip comes in, saying to look in the van behind Peterson's Ice Cream shop. I was working the swing shift; everyone else was busy assisting with the search efforts. So, I drive up the alleyway behind Peterson's, and I see Peterson's van, the van the anonymous caller identified, and I get out and walk over and peer inside the window. The windows aren't tinted, so I can see perfectly inside, and lying on the floor of the van is a pair of blue shorts and a yellow tank top. The same ones Linda Martin described her daughter was wearing the day she disappeared.

"I walked around to the front of the store, it was still morning, and the Ice Cream shop Peterson's had just opened but was still empty. Behind the counter was Mr. Peterson, the owner of the Ice Cream shop. I entered the store and asked him about the clothes in his van, and I asked him about Jennifer.

"Without missing a beat, he swears he doesn't know anything about the clothing in the van but offers that we should go out back and take a look. Maybe it belongs to his daughter, he answers. As he comes around the counter, Peterson pulls a handgun on me and begins firing the gun in my direction. I was scared shitless, but amazingly Peterson is an awful shot, and the bullets all miss me. In the heat of being shot at, I pull my service weapon and shoot him three times center mass, killing him. Peterson drops dead in a pool of his own blood.

"Long story short, the little girl Jennifer is never found. I become a hero in name only as the town is happy to be rid of a pedophile. But inside, in my heart, not knowing what happened to that girl Jennifer still haunts me to this day. The effects of Peterson abducting Jennifer spiraled and branched out effecting his family too.

"Peterson was also a single father, his little girl was taken by family services, and she is relocated to somewhere out west, Minnesota or Michigan. Searching the Peterson house and his van reveals no new leads to Jennifer's whereabouts. Peterson's daughter, probably suffering a lifetime of sexual abuse at the hands of her father, can't provide any information and is never heard from again. The fallout from the shooting makes me infamous here, and I quickly fall in with the town council, who, of course, see that I am chosen as the next Chief of Police." Browning said, taking another sip of his Pepsi and finishing the drink to the ice.

"My God, the things we have to live with," McNamara responded.

"Cape May is funny. There's a busy season where there's more work a person can possibly endure for about four months, and the rest of the time, you are chasing farts in the wind, chasing lost pets, taking domestic complaints, and issuing traffic citations. But overall, it's a good town, the summers are wonderful, and I will miss most of the people. But not so much that I won't retire." Browning said, wiping his mouth with a napkin and throwing the trash on the table before reaching into his wallet for some spare singles.

"Another piece of advice, John, always overtip when you eat in town. You don't want the townspeople talking behind your back about how much of a tightwad their new Chief of Police is." Browning suggested leaving the tip of singles on the table.

October 26, 2022

Thursday 3:26am

Eddie Wagner put his wool red, striped plaid hat on his head. Pulling the two ear guards down, Eddie tied the strap underneath his chin together so the ear guards would stay close to the sides of his face. His son Tommy stumbled out of the house in the dark, holding the thermos of coffee.

At seventeen years of age, Tommy was a typical teenager, no longer wanting to be seen with either of his parents and still wanting to sleep in on school days instead of chugging along with his father in the early blistery October mornings. Getting into the Queen Ocean Blue Z71 Double Cab Silverado, Tommy placed his head on the car's side window and went back to sleep while his father drove off of

W. Lake Drive and turned onto Lighthouse Ave, making the quick right in the dark onto Harvard.

A few blocks away, the light cast by the Cape May Lighthouse went out into the distance, rotating the white illumination into the surrounding seas. Pulling up to the nearest beach entrance, Eddie parked the Silverado truck and tapped his son on the shoulder.

"Get the other side." That was all Eddie said, and his son remaining in a still sleeping stupor, obliged by getting out of the passenger side.

Going to the front of the Silverado, Eddie and Tommy began letting the air out of the tires. Tommy, his son, no longer enjoyed coming along with his old man Eddie thought. The world has changed too much for kids these days. There are too many distractions now: cell phones, technology, school, sports, and of course, girls. How could he possibly compete with puberty? When Tommy was younger, he would beg to go fishing with him, just as Eddie had begged his father when he was little. Those days had disappeared, and now he was the one bothering his son for pieces of spare time.

This would all end soon, Eddie thought. Next year Tommy would go to college. He was already being recruited for two Division one schools to play different sports, baseball, and football. He was a man now, and next year at this time, his son would forget the days when his father woke him up to spend some time before work or school to take a few hours to fish on the beach. It was time they needed to spend together. There was still some time to hang onto before his son left home and become a man. Some more fleeting time to bond. One day when Eddie was no longer around, his son would never forget those early morning fishing trips with his father.

Eddie thought to himself, placing the plastic cap back on the tire wheel after letting the air out.

"How are we looking over there?" Eddie asked his son.

"Just finished," Tommy answered as both men climbed back into the truck's cab. Eddie put the car in four-wheel drive and drove over the pebbled sand, carefully avoiding the wood posting fence outlining the pathway down the beach. Going down the beach, with the beam from the lighthouse sweeping out to the sea, Eddie kicked up the sand on the shore of Lincoln Ave before parking perpendicular to Surf Ave and Cape Ave. The Silverado's headlights jetted out the truck's front cab with its high beams shining out to the sea.

Eddie and Tommy got out of the truck; they had done this routine hundreds of times together, each knowing their particular responsibility. Eddie would remove the cooler, tactical boxes, and beach chairs, while Tommy would attach the lures to the fishing rods, carefully ensuring the fishing reels and lines were threaded through the bait. Tommy had been doing this since his father had taught him at five years old, and even on a cold dark night with a gusting wind coming from the sea, Tommy could prepare the rods with his eyes closed.

"Need any help with that?" The thought and statement were polite, knowing there was never any need for assistance. Tommy's work was always impeccable. Coming over to inspect his son's work was simply a sign of approval. Checking over the rod, reel, lure, and bait in the Silverado's headlights, Eddie snapped back the rod and let the fishing line fly out to sea. Eddie placed the rod's handle in the folding chair's front attachment between his legs. His son Tommy followed suit and let the line go out farther than his father's before holstering the rod and taking a seat in the chair next to his father's.

The two men, father, and son, sat beside one another in the cold, neither breaking the silence with unnecessary words. Eddie poured a cup of the still steaming coffee for his son out of the thermos without being asked. Both took turns sipping the warm brew on their lips, allowing the beverage to warm their lips and color their faces against the blowing wind.

What felt like an eternity had passed before his father opened the dialogue.

"Have you given any thought about who you are taking to homecoming? It's next week, isn't it?" Eddie asked, and after a short pause, his son answered.

"I don't think I'm going?" Tommy answered.

"Why not? I thought you were still hanging out with Clarke's daughter; what is her name Kristy? She seemed nice and very pretty. Are you not seeing her anymore?"

"No. I mean, we hang out still, but how do I put this. Bitches be crazy." Tommy said, and his father laughed.

"Yes. I can definitely agree bitches can be crazy. Just don't tell your mother I said so." Eddie said, joining Tommy for a laugh.

"You see, dad, Kristy never wanted me for a boyfriend. She said because we are going to separate colleges next year, getting involved seriously with one another would only complicate things, and we would only end up getting hurt." Tommy explained.

"That's a very adult point of view from a seventeen-year-old," Eddie answered.

"Yea, so there is a girl. Pamela, she's a junior, and on the cheerleading squad, we sort of started hanging out together. I like her, but I also like Kristy." Tommy said.

"So, the question is, which girl do you ask to go with you to Home Coming?" Eddie asked.

"No. Not all. You see, if I invite Kristy, Pamela will find out and end things. She won't want to be second fiddle to another woman. But on the other side, Kristy won't speak with me or want to hang out if I invite Pamela." Tommy answered.

"So, it's a catch-22. No matter who you invite, either way, you lose." Eddie replied.

"Not necessarily. There is a third option. I don't go; neither Pamela nor Kristy gets hurt, and neither finds out about the other. Everything stays status quo." Tommy explained.

"Can you continue juggling both of them?" Eddie asked.

"I can, but they are both already buying dresses for Home Coming expecting me to take them. I haven't committed or asked either of them to go. So, like I said, bitches be crazy." Tommy said.

"That's a big problem to have. I wish you luck figuring it all out." Eddie said.

"Aren't you going to tell me what to do?" Tommy asked.

"No. I think my experience with women pales in comparison with yours, which makes me a little envious of your position. Besides..." As Eddie was finishing his sentence, the reel between his legs began to spin faster. Eddie placed the hammer lock down, picked up the reel, and started cranking and pulling on the fishing rod.

"That's got to be a big sucker. It's heavy." Eddie said, struggling.

After minutes of watching his father pulling and cranking on the fishing reel, Tommy took the steel green net down to the ocean, already having his plastic coveralls and matching boots on tread into the waves of the water, only to yell back to his father.

Eddie couldn't hear what his son was saying over the crashing waves, howling of the wind, and his own struggles with the behemoth on the other end of the fishing line. His son Tommy ran back up the beach to where his father continued his battle.

"Dad, I don't think it's a fish. I think your line got caught in a piece of sea timber." Tommy speculated, taking a knife from his pocket. Tommy was ready to cut his father's line.

"I don't think that's sea timber. It may be something else. Something bigger, something round." Eddie strained, staring out into the ocean; through the headlights of the Silverado, Eddie could make out the top of a curved black object bobbing up and down.

"Don't cut the line; go back out there, but not above your waist, and see if you can't help me pull whatever is out there in, will you," Eddie said, ordering his son.

Eddie's arms and back ached and burned with the mounting fight put up by the object floating toward the shore attached to the fishing line. He could see his son grab ahold of the floating object, pulling the thing with both arms, and walk backward whatever his lure had snagged. Eddie clipped the fishing wire when his son was just upon the shore and released the fishing pole. Taking a breath and resting his arms on his legs, Eddie could see his son waving in the light produced by the Silverado.

Trekking through the sand, Eddie could now see the object he fought to pull in from the sea, a wooden truck, no bigger than four feet by three feet.

"The box is heavy, dad. Help me push it up the beach." Tommy yelled, and Eddie obliged by getting with his son behind the trunk, and both father and son pushed the chest up the wet sand to the drier sand. The box slid through the wet sand, sinking deeper and deeper on the shore. The men adjusted their positions, switching from pushing to pulling when the tide stopped ebbing, and the wet sand turned to dried white sand. The trunk was no longer sinking into the sand, but the friction from the lack of water halted all progress of moving the heavy steamer any further up the shore.

Both men were panting with exhaustion, out of breath, and physically spent from the trial. The sea had put a task out, and the men had responded victorious in retrieving their trophy.

"Dad, it's pirate treasure. Just like in the movies, we're going to be rich!" Tommy proclaimed.

"We don't know what this is yet. Tommy, go and get the toolbox from the back of my flatbed."

Tommy ran up to the Silverado, reached into the steel-carrying load, and produced the toolbox, looking back at the shoreline where his father was kneeling down in the sand, looking over the trunk before running back to him.

Eddie was holding in his hand a key-operated steel padlock attached to the end of the clasp of the trunk.

"I don't think pirates shopped at the local hardware store for their locking devices," Eddie said holding the padlock. Opening the toolbox, Eddie felt the inside by hand, finding a wooden hammer with a steel balled head and a flat head screwdriver.

"Move off to the side, so I can see what I'm hitting in the light," Eddie instructed his son. As Tommy moved off to the side, Eddie placed the flat head screwdriver against the trunk clasp, using it as a chisel against the outer rim of the trunk's metal latch. The steel lock was still sturdy, but the wood surrounding the latch was weakened from its time spent in the sea. Eddie began pounding on the warped wood around the latch, taking the hammer, and cutting the rusted clasp away from the rest of the trunk.

After several strikes of the hammer meeting the makeshift chisel, the clasp broke and splintered free as the upper latch broke free from the lower lock of the trunk. With Tommy and Eddie standing on both sides of the chest, anxious to see what spoils lay inside. Father and son simultaneously opened the lid of the trunk and were met with a pair of white eyes staring up and through the two men.

***

"Do you know what time it is?" Browning asked, yawning into the telephone.

"I didn't think this could wait." The female dispatcher who worked the overnights said. Browning had forgotten her name before remembering it. Emily Thatcher. She had worked for the Cape May County Police for eight years as an overnight dispatcher. Eight years and Browning had only spoken to her a few times over those years. Thatcher, the Dispatcher, is how her co-workers referred to her.

"Well, what is it?" Browning demanded, turning the overhead light on the table beside his bed.

"A body was found by some local fisherman about thirty minutes ago near the light house. The first on the scene was Billy Preston. Billy said I should call you." Thatcher said.

"Did someone drown? Do we have an identification on the deceased?" Browning asked, sitting up in his bed, rubbing the sleep away from his eyes.

"Mr. Gilbert Epson, his wife, reported him missing yesterday morning. I also would hesitate to use the words drown. He was found locked inside a steamer trunk." Emily added.

"Shit, I spoke with his wife Danielle this afternoon, she's going to flip her wig when she hears her husband's dead, and because this is a small town, it's likely she already knows. Fuck." Browning sighed, thinking to himself as he sat in the bed.

"Ok. Call the coroner from Cape May. Have him meet me... where was the trunk found again?"

"On the beach in front of the Historic Light House. Just about Lincoln Ave," Thatcher responded.

"Ok, call the coroner from Cape May County. He should be on the weekly response sheet. Then call and wake up those two dickless detectives, Mattis and Brown, and tell them to borrow a forensics team from the county. Have them meet me over there. Call back Preston and have him detain whoever found the body for questioning, and any other responding units are to block off the streets surrounding Surf Ave and Cape Ave. We don't want unnecessary photographs to leak their way to the news."

"Got it," Thatcher said.

"Oh, and one more thing, call the new Chief McNamara and have him meet me there as well. He's staying at Congressional Hall."

"Understood," Thatcher replied as Browning hung up his cell phone. Couldn't this incident with Gilbert Epson waited just one more month? Browning thought to himself as he got up from the bed and walked to the shower stripping his bed clothing off on the floor as he turned the hot water up and let the steady stream wake him up.

Browning learned a long time ago the dead body was not going anywhere, and as the Chief of Police, they would wait on him to arrive.

October 26, 2022

Thursday 7:45am

Browning was standing on the upper wooden deck of the observatory in the parking lot of the Light House, watching the still-rising sun rise over the horizon. Less than two hundred yards from where the solid concrete World War II bunker used to detect potential Nazi submarines was left abandoned to rot on the beach. The bunker was now an empty relic of a forgotten age, sitting out of place on the beach like the Pyramids in the sand in Egypt as the twelve-foot-high smooth concrete structure was now covered with graffiti.

Down the beach and to the right, a line of yellow caution tape and vehicles surrounded the trunk washed up on the shore and the deceased body of Gilbert Epson. Forensic examiners, detectives, and uniformed officers milled around the crime scene while the coroner's van was loaded with Epson's remains. Despite all the movement, Browning was staring past the scurrying men and out to the sea, lost deep in thought as McNamara walked through the protected wetlands trail and up the wooden steps of the large observatory deck approaching Browning, who paid no attention to the visitor.

Browning felt melancholy and numb, ignoring the presence of the visitor on the observatory deck. Time was running out for him here in Cape May and despite the death Gilbert Epson Browning could only think of himself in this moment. It was selfish to think this way, comparing the end of his career with the death of a man he knew for years. But there it was.

"I understand it was Gilbert Epson they found in the box. I am sorry about the loss of your friend." McNamara said apologetically.

"Friend? That sorry sack of bones hadn't spoken to me in over ten years. Even when we sat on the council together, we were never that close. Any dealings we had were always mutually beneficial to one another for the benefit of the Township." Browning added without turning to look at McNamara.

"What now?" McNamara asked.

"Now we let the Mattis and Brown who couldn't find a lost bicycle do what they were hired to do. Investigate." Browning said.

"Is there any evidence?" McNamara asked.

"The coroner believes Epson was only out at sea for a day, maybe two days tops, which fits in with his wife's story about the time he went missing. We'll have to see her and break the news of his death. I am not looking forward to speaking with her. The old bat wouldn't stop pestering me yesterday when I went to talk with her. I can only imagine how much blame she'll assign my way."

"Did any other evidence turn up on Epson's body?" McNamara asked.

"There were some obvious puncture marks on Epson's neck suggesting he might have been drugged. Epson wasn't shackled inside the trunk, and there were no signs of struggle or damage where Epson was kept. There were sixty-plus pounds of chain link found inside the trunk with him, but he wasn't bound. The coroner believes he was drugged and possibly coherent about what was happening around him but helpless to defend himself. The coroner will know more after completing an autopsy and full pathology." Browning said.

Taking a walk and leaning on the rail next to Browning, McNamara looked out at the crime scene and the surrounding beach and sea.

"Enough putting this morning off; let's go talk to the widow," Browning sighed.

McNamara and Browning approached the front wrap-around porch with matching white rocking chairs of the two-story residence belonging to the now deceased Gilbert Epson.

"Are you any good at these?" Browning asked.

"Good at what? Telling people their loved one has died. No." McNamara said.

"I've avoided doing these for a large part of my career. How many have you done on the job?" Browning asked.

"More than I care to remember. One piece of advice I can give you is to get inside the house's front door. Ask to come in. You don't want her falling down or passing out in the doorway. It's better if she's sitting down." McNamara explained.

"I'll try to remember that" Browning said, putting his hat on his head and straightening the collar of his shirt under his jacket before ringing the doorbell.

Before the doorbell chiming could cease, Danielle Epson answered the door with her short, curled hair and wearing her pink sweat suit with matching pink slippers. Seeing Browning and McNamara at the door, her expression and the surprised look on her face changed to concern.

"She already knows." Browning thought to himself before the words could come from him and his mouth opened, but no sounds could come out. It was then McNamara cut in before Browning could speak.

"Mrs. Epson, we have some information concerning your husband. May we come inside for a moment?" McNamara said.

Moving aside, Danielle Epson allowed Chief's McNamara and Browning inside her home and into the living room. A large round glass table was in the center of the often-used room, while the sofa and matching green and white chairs were covered in plastic. It looked like your typical grandparent's house, Browning thought. Taking a seat in the center of the sofa, Danielle Epson looked at the two men standing.

"Can I offer you two something to drink?" Danielle Epson offered.

"No, thank you, Mrs. Epson. I regret to inform you that your husband was found deceased this morning. I am sorry for your loss." McNamara apologized. It was better to be out with it, to rip the band-aid off quickly, than to beat around the proverbial bush.

"Gilbert. Not Gilbert, no." Epson's hand went to her mouth in shock and sobs of tears as she repeated her dead husband's name out loud. The two men stood there, and McNamara nodded to Browning. Receiving the not-so-subtle gesture,

Browning went and sat down on the plastic next to Danielle, offering his shoulder to cry on, and Mrs. Epson held his jacket, laying her face on his shoulder.

"Why? Why? Why oh, why, my Gilbert." Danielle Epson continued her sobbing into the jacket of Chief Browning.

"Mrs. Epson, I know this is a terrible moment for you and your family. Is there anyone you would like us to call? Someone like a family member who can be here with you?" McNamara suggested.

"No. Helen, our only daughter, lives with her husband and grandchildren in Galveston, Texas. We were supposed to fly down there in the next few weeks and spend time." Danielle Epson said, releasing her grip on Browning's shoulder and wiping the tears from the sides of her deep red eyes.

"I want to write down our number. It's the Chief's personal number, our department will have some questions, and I'm sure you'll have some questions you want answered as well." McNamara looked around the room for a notepad and saw a yellow packet of sticky notes beside the telephone.

"How did he die? How did my husband die?" Danielle Epson asked.

"Preliminary evidence suggests he drowned Mrs. Epson. I know that doesn't make things any easier." Chief Browning answered, leaving out the trunk and injection marks on his neck.

"Drown? But that doesn't make any sense. My husband practically grew up in the Atlantic Ocean. He was a lifeguard when he was younger. He was a strong swimmer; how could he drown?" Mrs. Epson questioned them.

"You seem to follow what we are not saying to you, Mrs. Epson. We suspect foul play. When was the last time you spoke with your husband?" Browning asked, but before Mrs. Epson could answer, McNamara's cell phone began to ring.

"I have to take this. If you will excuse me for just a minute." McNamara excused himself and walked onto the porch, where Browning could see him through the large bay window.

"When I last spoke to my husband, it was Tuesday night. He was working late closing up the marina for the season. He said he had some paperwork to finish up and that his sister was ill, and he was considering seeing her." Mrs. Epson detailed as McNamara walked back inside the living room.

"Is there anything else you could tell us? Did he have any enemies? Receive any threats? Was there anything preoccupying his mind? You know, stressing him?" Browning asked.

"No, not that I am aware of. Gilbert never was one to stress very much about anything. He had a doctor's appointment a few months ago, and the doctor told him he was the healthiest sixty-seven-year-old he'd ever met." Mrs. Epson explained as tears started to swell. "And now he's gone."

"I am so sorry, Danielle, I really am. Please call me if there's anything I can do or something you can remember. A few detectives will follow up in a couple of days." Browning said, patting her on the back before getting up, trying not to rush for the door.

"I'll give my Helen a call. No doubt she'll rush up here in a hurry. I almost wonder if I should let her know at the end of the day. It's almost polite to break bad news at the end of the day, don't you think?" Mrs. Epson rhetorically asked as Browning stood silent, not answering, unaware of how early in the morning it still was. Just now realizing his workday had begun hours ago.

"My condolences again, Danielle. I'll get you more information when we know more." Browning said as he walked through the front door and a huge weight lifted off his shoulders as the door closed behind him.

Getting into the car with McNamara, the two men were silent for a few minutes neither discussing the conversation with Mrs. Epson until McNamara broke the ice.

"She may have been the last person who spoke with Mr. Epson," McNamara offered.

"Maybe. Subpoena the phone records for Gilbert Epson's cell phone and the marina. It would be nice to know who Mr. Epson spoke with or if another call was made after he spoke with his wife." Browning directed.

"Ok."

"Who was the call from?" Browning asked.

"Call?" McNamara asked.

"Yes, the call you left to take when we were talking with Mrs. Epson," Browning asked.

"Sorry. I almost forgot to tell you we need to go to the Cape May County Hospital. We have a hit on our mystery, Jane Doe, in the hospital." McNamara responded.

"Already? That was quick. She must have been in the system." Browning replied.

"Kind of sort of. Yesterday, when I left you, I drove to Hamilton's New Jersey State forensics laboratory. At the front desk is a gorgeous blonde; her last name is Christmas. No, I am not making any of this up. Her first name is January, and we get to some small talk, and we both start flirting with each other. I ask her, since when does January come before Christmas. She says, 'Oh, I've never heard that one before,' and rolls her eyes, but she hangs in there and asks me whether it is usual for a Chief of Police to drop off a DNA and fingerprint set, especially all the way from Cape May. I told her it was an important case and needed to be expedited. She says the fingerprints could come back soon, but the DNA results could take a couple of weeks because there is a waitlist." McNamara added with a grin.

"And?" Browning asked.

"The call was from January Christmas on her personal cell phone number. She moved us to the front of the waitlist. Next of kin were notified, and they should be able to meet us at the hospital when we get there."

"Anything else?"

"Yea, before I hung up, I told her Christmas came early in October," McNamara said.

"That is such a corny line. It's a cliché of a bad joke. Really, I can't believe you said that." Browning said, shaking his head.

"It is a corny line...er...was a corny line, but January responded, 'Christmas hasn't come in October yet," McNamara laughed, smiling and looking at Browning.

"Just drive. I can't be with you today, I'm inside with a grieving widow, and you're outside telling dirty jokes. Unreal the luck some guys have." Browning said as the Interceptor passed over the Cape May County bridge.

October 26, 2022
Thursday 9:20am

Clyde Browning and Joseph McNamara rode the elevator to the same floor they had been on the previous day. This time however it was Dr. Stannis and another man engaged in a conversation they found standing outside the hallway door of Jane Doe when the elevator door was pushed open. Doctor Stannis stopped his conversation to acknowledge the two Chiefs of Police and met them as they exited the elevator.

"Dr. Stannis." Chief Browning said as he exchanged handshakes with the doctor, and McNamara followed suit.

"Gentlemen, we were lucky. This is the son of my neighbor Dr. Bryan McDonough; he is the psychologist I recommended to treat Jane Doe. He was available to come and assist us this morning in the event when she hears her name there is a need..." Dr. Stannis said, losing the words.

"In case there is a need for a professional opinion. I'm only here to observe unless needed." Dr. McDonough added with a smile.

"Your parents live on Madison, don't they? I've known your father and mother for years. I don't remember you, though." Browning said, shaking hands with the psychologist.

"Yes, but they no longer live here in Cape May. My parents are retired in Florida now. I reside in their house now, but I do remember you, Chief Browning. You used to come to our school on career day and speak to us in the gymnasium when we were little children." Dr. McDonough said.

"So, what is the plan then?" Dr. Stannis asked.

"I'm going to walk into her room and tell Jane Doe her name. Hopefully, some kind of memory is stirred. Her next of kin, parents, should have been notified by dispatch already. If the memory of her name still eludes her, maybe seeing some familiar faces will jar some kind of reaction." McNamara speculated.

"Should we wait for the parents to arrive?" McNamara asked the psychologist.

"No. I don't think that's necessary. I believe we can proceed." Dr. McDonough answered. Chief

Browning and McNamara entered the room of Jane Doe, followed by Doctors Stannis and McDonough. Jane Doe was sitting upright in her bed watching television, and when she saw the two Chiefs of Police followed by two Doctors, she clicked the remote putting the television on mute.

"Back so soon." Jane Doe smiled as the four men huddled in the small solitary room.

"I have good news. The results from your DNA swab yesterday came back quicker than expected." McNamara said.

"Ok, what's the result?" Jane Doe asked.
"Your name, according to the New Jersey DNA Database, is Jennifer Martin," McNamara said. "Does that name ring any bells?"

"Wait. What?" Chief Browning interrupted.
"Excuse me, Chief?" McNamara said.

"The name you said, what was the name you just said?" Browning exclaimed cutting off the conversation.

"Her name is Jennifer Martin. Her DNA test results came back quickly because she was listed as missing. I thought you would be relieved to hear that she's been found alive after all these years." McNamara remarked to Browning.

"Jennifer Martin disappeared almost thirty years ago. I worked on that case. There is no way...no way...this could be that, Jennifer Martin. Child to Linda and Craig Martin. Jennifer Martin, in that case, died at the hand of a pedophile I killed.

There's no way this is that missing child." Browning protested as perspiration ran down both sides of his face.

"Chief Browning, is everything alright?" Dr. McDonough asked.

"No, everything is not alright. I'm telling you there must be some kind of mistake. An accident where the DNA results got mixed up. That is not Jennifer Martin." Browning snapped.

"Chief, why don't you have a seat while we ask Mrs. Martin if her name rings any bells or if she has some recollection of hearing that name. What about it, Jennifer? Do you remember being called Jennifer or Jen Martin?" Dr. McDonough asked the patient in the hospital bed.

"My name is Jen Martin. Jennifer Martin. No. I'm sorry, I don't recall ever using that name. Why is the Chief of Police adamant that I'm not Jennifer?" Jennifer asked.

"It's a long personal story for the Chief who was heavily invested in helping to find you all those years ago," McNamara informed her.

"Have you gained any memories, feelings, or intuitions about anything since being brought here, Jennifer?" Dr. McDonough asked.

"No, I'm sorry. I heard you mention my parents. What happened to them? What happened to my parents, Chief McNamara?" Jennifer asked.

"This must be some sort of joke, Clyde." The woman's voice from behind the men scoffed.

As the men turned to look at the doorway, a thin older woman in her late fifties stood at the entrance to the room.

"I'm sorry. Who are you?" McNamara asked.

"Linda Martin. I received a telephone call from one of the dispatchers that my daughter was found and here in the hospital. I assumed they meant the morgue and wanted me to identify a body. Instead, I was directed up to this room." Linda Martin explained.

"Oh, Mrs. Martin. It pleases me to inform you that your daughter has been found alive after all these years." Dr. McDonough said with a smile extending over his cheeks.

"Poppycock!" Linda Martin exclaimed.

"Excuse me. I know your feelings must be overwhelming at this moment, but according to DNA results, this is your daughter Jennifer." McNamara reaffirmed.

"I may be older, but I did not grow stupid, feeble minded or blind. Do any of you think I would not be able to recognize my own daughter? That woman in that bed is not my daughter." Linda Martin stated.

"That's what I told them, Linda. It can't be her." Browning chimed in.

"Clyde, I don't know what this is all about, but if it turns out, you had something to do with it." Linda threatened.

"I just found out right before you walked in. I'm so sorry, Linda, for you to relive this." Browning said.

"Where's my daughter?" A man's voice cried as the door to the room opened. An older man with heavy-rim glasses carrying a cane and a full head of sea salt hair entered the room.

"Mr. Martin? Your daughter is in bed." McNamara said.

"My Jennifer. Jen." The older man moved to the hospital gurney. "Let me get a good look at you." Mr. Martin said, fighting back his tears as he sat on the bed.

"I'm so sorry, sweetheart...I failed you all those years ago...I'm sorry." The old man Martin sobbed, hugging Jennifer Martin and crying into her blonde hair.

"Mr. Martin?" Dr. McDonough said, trying to gain his attention through the swelling tears.

"Yes. Hello Linda and Clyde." Craig Martin answered, turning to the two other people he recognized in the room as he wiped the tears from under his eyes.

"Mr. Martin, I'm Dr. McDonough, a psychologist brought in to assist Jennifer in regaining her memories. You see, she is suffering from retrograde amnesia."

"How bad is her memory?" Craig Martin asked, still holding his adult daughter in his arms.

"She has no recollection of anything before being found on the Cape May bridge a few nights ago." Dr. McDonough informed him.

"Oh, you poor thing." Craig Martin said, turning to his daughter.

"Mr. Martin, there seems to be some dispute as to whether this is Jennifer. The DNA tests confirm it's her, but Chief Browning and your wife enthusiastically claim it's not her." Dr. McDonough said.

"Ex-wife." Craig Martin snorted.
"Excuse me?" McNamara asked.

"She's, my ex-wife. It doesn't surprise me she doesn't recognize her own daughter. Of course, this is Jennifer." Craig Martin refuted, turning back to the woman he was holding in the bed. "God's answered my prayers and brought you back to me. When can I take her home Doctor?"

"I didn't realize all your devotional work over the years drove you, senile Craig. That woman is an imposter. It's not Jennifer. You may hate me, but deep down, you know that's not our Jennifer." Linda Martin rebutted.

"You were responsible for her the day she disappeared. God is giving you a second chance, Linda, and you are too stubborn to accept that opportunity." Craig responded.

"Say what you want to yourself, lie to yourselves, parade her around as your daughter, and take all the DNA samples you need. But you will not bring me into this. That is not my daughter. I don't want to hear any more about this, so don't call me with any further nonsense. Am I making myself clear, Clyde Browning?" Linda Martin fumed before turning and stampeding out of the room.

"Jennifer, I know this must be very confusing for you. But seeing your mom and dad again, does this bring back any memories for you?" Dr. McDonough asked.

"I'm sorry, no. I don't remember either of my parents." Jennifer stated.

"It's alright, dear. We'll get through this together. You were young when you went missing. Pieces will come back in time. Won't they, Doctor?" Craig Martin asked, unsure.

"Yes. Yes, I believe there is an excellent chance her memories will come back. I also believe we should send Jennifer home unless Dr. Stannis has any objections. Maybe being back in Cape May and getting her mind situated or occupied will have the unintended consequence of bringing back some memories." Dr. McDonough recommended.

"Kind of like when you can't remember something until you put it aside. She may be trying too hard to remember." Dr. Stannis said in agreement.

"In the meantime, I would very much like to see Jennifer later this week. I believe hypnosis therapy or a tour of her old house or town could jog some distant memories." McDonough offered, reaching into his jacket pocket and producing a business card for Mr. Martin.

"My cell phone is listed. Please feel free to call me day or night with any questions." Dr. McDonough smiled.

"Thank you, Doctor. We'll call and set up an appointment for later this week." Craig Martin said.

"Well, gentleman, if there's nothing further, we should leave father and daughter alone to get reacquainted." Dr. McDonough said, ushering out the crew of men watching the reunion.

After thanking Dr. Stannis and Dr. McDonough for their time, Chief Browning and Chief McNamara got on the elevator.

"What in the fuck was that shit?" Browning snarled, turning to McNamara.

It was taking every once of self-control Browning possessed not to physically assault McNamara in the elevator. Browning stepped closer to McNamara and got face to face. Browning knew he was fuming and emotional, but how could McNamara lead him up to that room and ambush him with something so personal as the revelation that Jane Doe was Jennifer Martin? McNamara betrayed him and the hurt was fueling his emotions.

"What do you mean?" McNamara asked.

"You fucking blindsided me with that information. I told you yesterday about Jennifer

Martin, and this morning her name just turns up out of the fucking blue, and you forgot to mention to me that's who we are going to see. You must think I'm fucking stupid." Browning shouted as spit flew from his mouth.

"It was an honest mistake. We were so busy this morning breaking the news to Mrs. Epson. It just slipped my mind." McNamara said defensively.

"The next time something important slips your mind, you'll be the next one they pull out of the Atlantic Ocean. You understand me?" Browning threatened, pointing his index finger at McNamara.

"I don't understand," McNamara asked. "What don't you understand?"

"You and Mrs. Martin are adamant that's not Jennifer Martin in that hospital bed. Why is that? You would think you both would be happy to have a good ending to this story from thirty years ago?" McNamara asked.

"Get this through that thick head of yours. That is not Jennifer Martin upstairs in that hospital room. No way, no how. No matter how many DNA tests suggest it is, they are wrong. In fact, when we get back to the station, I want you to call your honey boo-boo back in Hamilton at the Forensics lab and ask her to re-run those results and, when she finishes checking them, to recheck them again." Browning fumed.

"Ok, I can do that, but what makes you so sure it's not Jennifer Martin?" McNamara asked before the elevator door opened.

"Drop the subject. Go back to the station and get me the test results. I'll get a ride back into town on my own." Browning commanded, storming from McNamara in the lobby.

October 26, 2022
Thursday 11:47pm

Beatrice Murphy sat perched at the window of her bedroom, staring through the dark night at the crashing waves from her third-floor room out past Harvard Ave. Insomnia. When she felt she could still be independent, Beatrice was forced to live with her daughter and husband in the affluent Cape May's historic area. Despite being seventy-five years old and in possession of all her faculties, she developed stomach cancer.

Now she lay awake at night, feeling she was a burden to her family and a failure to herself. As if there was some way of preventing cancer from occurring. Part of her nightly routine was staring out the window and looking across from her house onto the triangle piece of property occupied by Saint Peter's by the Sea Episcopal Church.

Beatrice had her window cracked, letting the breeze into her room, and a blanket pulled over her shoulders so she could smell the salt roll off the ocean and keep warm at the same time while listening to the crashing waves on the nearby shore. She sat alone in her room, the light from the bedside table behind her was muted as the late-night show did his monologue in the background.

Beatrice was scheduled for chemotherapy again in the morning. A driver would come and pick her up and drop her back off after the treatment was finished. The cancer treatment wore her out and numbed her to everything else, dulling her sense of life. Sometimes she thought about why she was prolonging the inevitable, the right to die with a sense of dignity.

"Was it right to prolong a life where all sense of enjoyment had passed?" Beatrice wondered as she stared into the darkness. The doctors assured her she would beat the cancer, but for the next year or two, the treatments would eat away at her, draining her life away.

Without being told by the doctors, Beatrice was aware of the increased likelihood that a second form of cancer would develop in the next few years if she beat the stomach cancer. Older and unable to have her immune system function from fighting off cancer the first time, her death would be hastened. The clock on her own demise and how she had lived her life kept her up at night worrying about events she could not control.

Looking out the window below to S. Lake Dr., a white van parked outside Saint Peter's by the Sea church sat idle with a cloud of white smoke emanating from the exhaust pipe.

"Odd that van should pull up outside at this time of night?" Beatrice thought to herself, staring down from the window, trying to catch a glimpse of the driver inside. Reaching next to the table with the remnants of her evening herbal tea, Beatrice pulled her binoculars to her eyes and began adjusting the wheel in the center to bring the van into focus.

The van sat center across from her bedroom, and while Beatrice didn't consider herself a Peeping Tom, the binoculars were considered by her an investment into community policing. A spur-of-the-moment purchase made at a flea market when she still had the energy to shop.

Of course, no one admits to being a snoop or a busybody. Even fewer people like having an old woman spy on them from the tallest house on Harvard Street. But occasionally, her sleuthing experiences paid off, such as what happened two summers ago when she saw the damage done to the Summertime church across the street by three teenage vandals.

At this time of night, to have an unfamiliar vehicle prowl around and park outside the church brought an uneasy feeling to Beatrice, a sense of Deja Vu.

At present, the vehicle was just sitting idle, a solitary van parked by itself, not much happening. Before calling the police, Beatrice would need more of a reason. What they called on those police shows "probable cause." The van could be two teenagers necking or doing more with one another in the back, or a simpler reason could be a night surfer who would use the Harvard beach entrance for night surfing. Neither of these possibilities could be ruled out, but the situation merited further attention.

The van's panel back doors swung open as Beatrice moved the dial on the binoculars into focus on the window cabin. A metal ramp clattered on the concrete below, echoing in the night as the ramp bounced off the street. A figure emerged, covered in a black cloak, backing down the ramp with a large metal hand truck. Situated on the hand truck Beatrice saw was a wooden cross with naked Jesus nailed on to it, tools and a can of gasoline sat next to the cross on the hand truck. The statue of Jesus on the Cross had a black knapsack covering his head.

It must be a delivery for the church, Beatrice thought initially. An uneasiness overcame her initial misgivings, something more nefarious was going on with the van. The uneasy feeling lingered, coming a second time, a more sinister feeling when looking at the clandestine-robed figure pushing the handcart past the white wooden fence and onto the Saint Peter's by the Sea property.

Why would a delivery take place at almost midnight? She asked again. Watching the figure dressed in black began to give Beatrice the creeps. Unable from her window to catch a glimpse of the robed delivery person's face, Beatrice saw something unmistakable occur as the Jesus on the Cross moved. She wasn't positive at first about seeing the movement. With the binoculars trained on the cross lying flat on the large handcart, she saw the person attached to the Cross was not Jesus Christ but a live person.

The handcart wheels locked into position, and the black-robed figure took the wooden post-hole digger, planted it into the frozen earth, and pulled up the ground below. The movement by the hooded figure dressed in black was quick, thrusting the metal shears into the ground and removing dirt while making the hole deeper.

With a lump in her throat and chills running over her body, Beatrice wanted to put the binoculars down and call the police, call anyone for help. She had to tell someone to make the figure working on the lawn of the Episcopal Church across the street stop. But like a movie playing on a projector, the picture would not stop, and the scene playing in front of her would not halt. No matter how much she wanted to, Beatrice could not tear herself away from watching the events unfolding across the street.

With the hole dug, the robed figure pulled the Cross of wood with the strapped person off the handcart and past the entrenched earth. The robbed figure lined the bottom of the wood Cross up with the hole, implanting the base into the cavity and sinking the Cross in the dug earth. The victim tied to the Cross was standing upright in the cold, and Beatrice could see breaths of cold air coming from under the hood permeating into the night air. As the dark, robbed figure planted the dug-out soil back into the hole to sturdy the surroundings of the upright Cross, Beatrice, through her open window, could make out a little of what the victim was saying. She didn't have to guess; he was begging, pleading for his life.

The robed figure reached onto the handcart removed the nozzle from the tiny red gasoline container and began pouring the liquid all over the man tied to the Cross. When the gasoline ran dry, a conversation developed between the robed figure dressed in black and the man tied to the Cross. At first, Beatrice assumed this was more begging from the victim, but through the open window, she swore she could hear a small amount of dialogue

"Tell me you are guilty. Tell me you have sinned. Confess." The robed figure asked.

"I'm guilty. I've sinned. Please spare me. I'll confess." The man on the Cross cried.

The robed figure dressed in black produced a matchbook and lit all the heads of the matchbook before throwing it at the pool of gasoline puddled into the frozen earth around the Cross. The streak of blue flame danced from the ground and up over the near-naked body of the person Beatrice initially thought was Jesus. Screams went out in the darkness as fire engulfed the sack drenched in petrol on the man's head.

In the blazing fire on the Cross and the burning flames, the robed figure turned toward the house Beatrice occupied, looked up through her third-floor window, and made eye contact with Beatrice staring down. The binoculars glued on her face provided a front-row seat to the act of murder that had just occurred.

For the first time, Beatrice and the robed figure sat eye to eye, and Beatrice identified who the murderer was, someone she had seen pictures of and had heard of since she was a little girl. Death itself was present. The robed figure three floors down, standing in front of the Church of Saint Peter's by the Sea, was the Grim Reaper himself. The Grim Reaper seeing Beatrice stare down from across the street, raised its hand and pointed its index finger at Beatrice, letting her know she had been identified as a witness to the murder.

***

Saint Peter's by the Sea church was originally moved to Cape May Point in Eighteen Seventy-Nine before being relocated four times to its present location on the triangle-shaped lot on Ocean Avenue and Lake Drive. The church but was initially located on Beach Avenue until its forced relocation due to the battery of the Atlantic Ocean reclaiming the buildings on the shore.

With several updates since the church's initial construction including a bell tower, pews, a lavatory, and the addition of a front porch from the eighteen-eighties to a new altar in nineteen sixty-five. The small church is closed through the winter and fall months opening only in the summertime and is best known throughout Cape May as the most photographed building in the borough. Tonight, the news crews and camera people would make Cape May's most famous landmark infamous.

Unlike the discovery of Gilbert Epson earlier in the day, where the crime scene could be contained, the location of the Saint Peter's by the Sea Church was problematically situated between three streets and then across a large sand wall to prevent the water from claiming other buildings inland. The location of the murder setup provided the paparazzi with clean camera angles in all directions.

Clyde Browning could only fume to himself. The wooden Cross had not burned through and was still standing upright, the smoking charred remains of the victim attached via chain link around the arms, legs, and torso sat upright exposed for all the news crews to film. In fact, the news crews had arrived almost simultaneous to his officers. Every minute the body remained propped up was an affront to Browning's sense of authority.

"Are we done processing the crime scene? Can we please take the body down?" Browning shouted to the forensic crime scene unit, looking for someone to authorize the body to be taken down.

"I think we have all we need. We can process the rest back at the laboratory." A diminutive woman wearing a CSI cap answered.

"Then cut him down. Cut him down!" Browning commanded, standing outside the wooden fence area at the end of the triangle corner, the smell from the corpse still sizzling in his nostrils. Detective Mattias walked over with Chief McNamara toward Browning. Mattias was clutching his notepad open while holding his jacket together in an effort to keep warm. McNamara was drinking from a disposable coffee cup, the steam still leaving the tiny slit in the top plastic piece.

"Give me something," Browning demanded, impatient for information.

"If you look behind us, up to the third-floor window of the wooden house, you will find the room of one Beatrice Murphy. Seventy-five years old, insomniac, and the best of all, she saw the whole murder." Mattias said, referring to his notes.

"That's great, so we have a description of the murderer," Browning remarked.

"Kind of sort of...." Mattias replied before McNamara cut him off.

"She described a white van, no license plates, some dialogue where the victim admitted to committing some type of crime before being torched," McNamara added.

"What about the suspect, White, Black, Asian, Old, Young?" Browning asked, getting impatient.

"It appears Halloween came early this month. The suspect was dressed...get this, as the Grim Reaper. The Reaper gave old Beatrice up there quite the fright when he pointed at her. The paramedics are sedating the old woman now so she can get some sleep." Mattias said.

"The Grim Reaper?" Browning asked for confirmation.

"Mrs. Murphy described a cloaked black figure which, when observed in the light coming from the burning Cross, had a skull for a face. The only item the Grim Reaper was missing was his scythe." Mattias continued.

"Do we have an identification on the John Doe hung up on the Cross?" Browning asked.

"Yes. Detective Brown called in when he was looking for the property owners. Reverend Mulvaney and his wife. After not receiving an answer on their home phone, he went to their residence and found Mrs. Mulvaney tied up. She appears to have been drugged with something similar to what was used on Mr. Epson this morning. Reverend Mulvaney was missing. Beatrice described the victim on the Cross as an older man with white hair on his chest, legs, and sagging skin. I believe the John Doe is Reverend Mulvaney." McNamara said.

"You got to be kidding me, Thomas Mulvaney? Fuck, he's been a prominent member of Cape May since the nineteen seventies." Browning said.

"When the press finds out it was the Pastor of Saint Peter's by the Sea who was burnt alive, they are going to have a field day with this," Browning said, running his fingers through his colored hair.

"Okay. This is what we are going to do; we need to get ahead of this. McNamara will hold an impromptu press conference, telling the press we are working on identifying the victim. Say something to the effect that we cannot rule out a hate crime at this time or that this murder is related to the body discovered this morning. If they have any questions, just answer with the phrase we are still conducting an investigation, and when we can release that information, we will." Browning ordered.

"Mattias put an APB out for any and all white vans. I want that van found and processed. Have your men go door to door and see if anyone else saw anything. This Grim Reaper description is lacking, to say the least. I'll get with Brown and have forensics go to the Mulvaney house dust for any hair fibers or fingerprints. I want the drug in Mrs. Mulvaney and Mr. Epson analyzed. What is the drug, where can one get it, and how hard is this drug to obtain? We are on the clock now. Tomorrow morning, we make the front page of every internet article and lead story on every channel's news station."

"Any questions? Then get on it, gentlemen. We have a killer to catch." Browning charged.

Browning watched as Mattias, and McNamara followed their orders as instructed. The crime scene unit was covering the burned body of Reverend Mulvaney while an officer clipped the steel chain links holding the victim to the wooden Cross. Neither Mattias nor McNamara had asked the most important question. If the murder of Epson and Mulvaney are connected, what is that connection?

October 27, 2022

Friday 7:04am

Linda Martin's internal clock went off this morning, the same as it had every morning for the last thirty years, at six-fifteen am. There was no use in setting a clock. The internal mechanisms of her brain were hard-wired on a set schedule for the last thirty years and were far more accurate than any clock. Even through time changes, her body would naturally adapt, and whether an hour ahead or behind, she was always awoken at six-fifteen.

Her routine was always the same, get up in the cold house as it was not chilly enough for the heat to be turned on in her opinion as of yet, climb into her yoga pants and North Face cardigan, rinse her mouth with antiseptic, take a few sips of water and begin stretching. Her stretching routine started with lunges, splits, and hamstring stretches before beginning her daily six-mile run down the concrete boardwalk on Beach Avenue, past the Cape May Convention Center and rows of endless hotels.

Despite being fifty-six years old, she still felt young. Linda could finish her first three miles on the promenade at just under eleven miles a minute. Always stopping at the end of the Beach Ave pavilion, Linda would stop regardless of the weather and take a breather. Across the street from The Cove Restaurant and Seaside Deck on the boardwalk pavilion is where Linda would stop and admire the rising sun or the moving clouds no matter what type was weather coming down.

This morning, Linda could see the Cape May County Light House in the distance, further on the World War II lookout tower and the closest building on the beach, the abandoned World War II bunker. Here Linda would say a quick prayer before resuming her run.

Completing the sign of the Cross, Linda was mouthing the first few words of the Lord's Prayer to herself.

"Our Father, who aren't in Heaven, hallowed be thy name."

"Funny, I never took you for the religious type." A man said to her.

Looking to her right, Linda saw Clyde Browning sitting in his Ford Police Interceptor, smiling at her.

"Morning, Clyde. What can I do for you?" Linda asked as she jostled back and forth, trying to stay loose and keep the lactic acid from cramping her legs up.

"Did you hear about last night? Reverend Thomas Mulvaney was killed. Put up on a Cross and lit on fire. Poof." Browning said, putting his fingers to his lips and blowing on them for an exaggerated effect when he uttered the word, Poof.

"Yes, all of Cape May has heard about that. I thought you were coming to talk to me about that girl in the hospital, the one impersonating my daughter." Linda replied.

"What would be the use of wasting my words talking to you about her? We both know that's not Jennifer." Browning said.

"Clyde, far be for me to speak out of turn in matters of your investigation, but have you stopped to consider these events aren't independent of one another?" Linda asked.

"How so?" Chief Browning asked.

"What I mean is I don't believe in coincidences. First, the death of Gil Epson, then Reverend Mulvaney, even an amateur could prove those deaths are connected. But I would wager that woman pretending to be my daughter. She's connected to these murders somehow. You know how they're connected. We both know how Jennifer and those two are connected. Pretending it didn't happen all those years ago, only muddies things." Linda said.

"The thought has crossed my mind. But then there's that damn DNA test and her father showing up and vouching that it was her." Clyde pointed out.

"Craig wouldn't have recognized Jennifer. You could have shown him any blonde woman. The chance to have his daughter back, to give back some of that guilt. Deep down, I always felt Craig knew about our involvement with one another." Linda refuted.

"Speaking about our involvement with one another, Linda, you know there are mornings I sit in Uncle Bill's Pancake House, and I watch you run by on the boardwalk in the morning, and I reminisce about old times. I am leaving soon, Linda, retiring to Key West to do a lot of fishing, maybe write the novel I keep putting off, and drink a lot. But mostly, I will forget about this place and move on. I could use some company when I go down there, and I think you could use a reset on your life too. Would you go with me, Linda?" Clyde asked.

"Browning, I don't have time to entertain your fantasies. Hell, we haven't even spoken about that in almost thirty years. I am perfectly content here in Cape May." Linda said.

"Linda, you haven't been content since the day Jennifer disappeared. We were happy once, you and I, it may have been brief, but I always carried a flame for you, thought about you even if I was with someone else. There's nothing I wouldn't do for you then. I believe the same goes for me now." Clyde proposed.

"Your offer is flattering, Clyde, it really is... but my life is here. I don't think I could ever go anywhere else." Linda said.

"Ok, Linda, I thought I would ask one last time," Clyde said, starting to roll up his window.

"Clyde," Linda said, stepping off the concrete promenade down to the sidewalk as Clyde glanced sideways toward her.

"Clyde. I meant what I said about coincidences. There's no way that amnesic woman in the hospital and those deaths aren't related. My question to you is, what else has happened, that has been too much of a coincidence lately? Don't answer me; just think about it and then do something about it. Be safe." Linda said, climbing up the nearby stairs and resuming her run back to her house.

Looking in the rearview mirror Chief Browning already had an answer to Linda's question. Yes, there was something too good to be true.

Congress Hall, the hotel McNamara was staying in was originally built in eighteen sixteen as a boarding house with sparse living conditions. Until eighteen twenty-eight when its owner, Thomas H. Hughes, was elected to Congress, changing the name from "The Big House" because of the large number of rooms to Congress Hall. A rich history of past presidents who vacationed at Congress Hall included Ulysses S. Grant, James Buchannan, Franklin Pierce, and Benjamin Harrison. In two-thousand one, an extensive renovation was completed putting Congress Hall into the fabled and exquisite state vacationers currently enjoy.

McNamara had told Browning he had received a generous discount for lodging at Congress Hall through the winter but would need to find other accommodations by May. It was a win for both Congress Hall in gaining favor with the new Chief of Police by allowing him to reside there and for Congress Hall to have an income throughout the slower winter months when tourists visited Cape May for the day but rarely spent the night.

Browning went to the front desk and was greeted by the receptionist. A petite blonde female with her name tag reading Sara.

"Welcome to the Congress Hall, Chief Browning. What can I do for you?" Sara asked.

She recognized me. That's a good start, Browning thought, who was still wearing his uniform.

"Do you happen to know if Chief McNamara returned here this morning? I was supposed to pick up some of my stuff from his room." Browning asked.

"I can call up to the room if you need me to?" Sara picked up the phone and dialed McNamara's room extension with no answer.

"I'm sorry, Chief, it doesn't appear he's in," Sara said, hanging up after a few rings.

"If you could give me the key to his room, I'll just need two minutes to grab my things," Browning assured her.

"Let me check with the manager. We are not supposed to give out keys to our guests' rooms to non-guests." Sara answered.

"I understand, but please ask," Browning said, not moving away from the desk. Browning could see Sara walk to her supervisor, the manager of Congress Hall, David Rodriguez. Rodriguez was a man who owed Browning. Over his career as Chief, several people found themselves in Browning's debt. In Rodriguez's case, he was caught drunk driving, intoxicated over twice the legal limit. An arrest and conviction would terminate his job as manager of Congress Hall.

On the morning after his intoxication arrest, Browning entered the cell where Rodriguez was sobering up and sat down next to him. The two men had never spoken before this moment, but a deal was struck. Browning stipulated certain favors rendered in the future in exchange, the machine reading Rodriguez's sobriety would be malfunctioning. No charges would be brought, and Rodriguez would be free to go, but those favors would need to be honored when called in.

Browning saw Rodriguez speaking with Sara, the receptionist, and the manager glanced at the front desk toward Browning, who nodded his ascent, a non-verbal cue. A favor was being called in. Sara returned, placed a plastic card into the reader on the desk, and after a brief moment, put McNamara's room key on the desk.

"Room two-twenty-four, Chief Browning," Sara said with a smile. Retrieving the key, Browning went to the nearest elevator, rode up to the second floor, walked to room two-twenty-four, and knocked on the door. With no response, Browning inserted the key card and entered the room. The room's décor was an antique decorated with yellow floral wallpaper. An older desk, bureau with mirror, a cabinet with a television insert, and a queen size bed with two side tables holding lamps on either end. A large spacious bathroom with a tub, shower, closet, and double vanity sink.

The room was neat, the bed made; other than the shaving razor and toothbrush, the room could have been mistaken as unoccupied. Browning wasn't sure what he was searching for but began on the side end tables, opening the shelves and pouring their contents on the floor, checking underneath the shelves before moving to the bed, flipping the mattress, and checking underneath the bed.

Moving to the television cabinet, Browning searched methodically behind the television and then, in the same manner as before, removed the drawers of clothing and emptied their contents onto the floor. Socks, underwear, slacks, and t-shirts fell to the floor. Rifling through the clothing Browning didn't discover anything more than McNamara preferred briefs over jockeys. Searching the room's air vents, Browning found them undisturbed, providing no clues.

Going to the desk, Browning removed the desk drawers with the contents belonging to the hotel, including pads of paper, menus, pens, and a large plastic binder of local attractions. Moving to the bathroom, Browning began his search in the closet; rows of pressed white shirts, slacks, and button-down navy-blue jackets hung fresh from the dry cleaners. Below the line of work clothes were McNamara's shoes. Browning took turns examining each shoe before tossing them back into the closet. Two empty gym bags were laid on the floor and revealed nothing untoward.

The search of the room was a bust. Browning sat at the desk and swiveled in the wooden chair staring at the mess he had made in the room. There was something he was missing; he was sure of it. His instincts as a policeman screamed at him, but Browning couldn't put his finger on what exactly he was missing despite this screaming instinct. Instead, Browning stared at the mess on the floor before picking up his cell phone and making a call.

***

It was almost ten before the electronic key lock to McNamara's room turned, and McNamara walked in. Seeing Browning sitting in his room at the desk with the contents of the room dumped out in a disorganized manner.

"What the fuck is going on in here? Why the fuck are you in my room?" McNamara yelled, pointing his finger at the still seated Browning.

"Whoa, whoa, whoa, calm down, calm yourself. I had to be certain." Browning replied.

"Certain of what?" McNamara yelled at him. "I had to be certain you weren't him," Browning said.

"Him who? The murderer, the Grim Reaper? Unfucking believable you are. If you even thought I was the murderer, there's a little thing known as a search warrant. I don't suppose you obtained one before trashing my room. Of course not. You've been a cowboy your whole life living here in Cape May with your own personal town to do with as you want. No one would question you. I'll tell you what, asshole, I'm going to bring you up in front of internal affairs." McNamara threatened.

"Internal Affairs, like you did at your last job in Minneapolis. I called your Chief over there this morning while I sat here." Browning said.

"You called Chief Morris about me?" McNamara asked.

"Yea, yea, I did. Chief Fields didn't care for you too much, ratting out your partners the way you did. You didn't exactly enamor yourself with anyone in the precinct there. That kind of label follows people. The only way out of the situation where they could get rid of you and have you kept quiet was another job, a promotion." Browning stated.

"That wasn't the way it went down," McNamara replied.

"Doesn't really matter, does it. Chief Fields said you were a stand-up officer. That's all I took from the conversation. A stand-up officer doesn't start killing people. There's no motive behind it, no rationale. That information and this search answers some of my questions." Browning said.

"What other questions could you have?" McNamara asked.

"Where were you this morning? Where did you go after the murder?" Browning asked.

"I drove back to Hamilton and the New Jersey State Forensics Laboratory. You asked me to double-check the DNA on Jennifer Martin and Jane Doe from the hospital."

"And?"

"And it's still a match. No change. Here's the paperwork." McNamara said, removing a paper from his top pocket and crumbling it up before throwing it at Browning.

"Do you have any other questions before I have your ass fired?" McNamara asked.

"You could do that. But I am out of here in less than thirty days anyway. Going to Internal Affairs and making an allegation would only waste the time we have left. You would be wasting people's time over something that will disappear when I hit the beaches of Key West." Browning replied.

"Okay, I'll let you off the hook, Browning, but I need to know something. In Biaggi's, there was a picture of five younger men sitting at a large table. You were in the picture, so was Biaggi, and so were the two dead men, Epson and Mulvaney. I know I don't qualify as a detective, but how do their deaths connect with you?" McNamara asked.

"I don't know yet," Browning answered.

"Ok. Answer me this, how were you so certain it wasn't Jennifer Martin in the hospital bed yesterday?" McNamara asked.

"I'll take you into confidence with this. Few people know. I was having an affair with Linda Martin when her daughter went missing. I went above and beyond to investigate every lead, working every waking second until that information came in, and I caught that sonnabitch who took her. When I caught him, I thought Linda and I would end up together, but she was shattered. I ended up only as a reminder of what had happened to her daughter. In a way, she blamed herself and me for Jennifer's disappearance. So, you see, I knew Jennifer well, really well. No matter what this DNA test says, I say it's not her." Browning said, turning and looking out the window.

"Any other questions? If not, maybe we can start to trust one another and build upon that." Browning said.

The two men, once face to face, gave each other some space, not saying anything as McNamara began picking up his clothes scattered on the floor and placing them back into the cabinet's drawers. Browning came over to help when his cell phone rang.

"What is it, Mattias?" Browning asked answering the phone.

"Sir, we have a lead on the white van." Detective Mattias said.

"Call Judge Adams, get an electronic search warrant. Let Adams know this is related to the two murders and have the warrant e-mailed to me. What's the location of the van? McNamara and I will be there in short order." Browning asked.

"That's the problem, sir. The van is at Officer Preston's house. Preston is inside, sleeping. He worked the overnight shift last night. The longer we wait, the more there is a chance of someone on the force calling Preston and letting him know we are on to him." Mattias said.

"Officer William Preston? Are you sure? I've known him for almost seventeen years. I'm pretty sure Preston doesn't own a white van. How did we come up with this information?" Browning asked.

"An anonymous caller called it in about thirty minutes ago," Mattias said.

"And you're sure the van is at Preston's house?" Browning asked again.

"I drove by to verify before calling you myself. I saw it there in the back inside the open shed garage area." Mattias answered.

"I want the warrant ready for when we get there or there will be hell to pay." Browning threatened hanging up the phone.

October 27, 2022
Friday 10:44am

Browning got behind the steering wheel of the Ford Interceptor, while McNamara got in the passenger side seat. Officer William Preston lived in a small two-bedroom cape home on Pennsylvania street.

"What did Mattias say?" McNamara asked.

"Mattias said he received an anonymous call directly to his cell phone. He called me right after he drove past Preston's house; the white van described by our victim was parked in Preston's garage with the garage door open.

Knowing how loose our department's lips are about secrets, he called me. I told him to call the Cape May Sheriff's office and have their tactical team block off the street Preston lives on. Our officers would provide support and not be informed of who the target is. Hopefully, no one wises up and calls Preston at home. He's armed and our only suspect."

"You don't seem to believe that Preston is the Grim Reaper. Why is that?" McNamara asked.

"I've known Preston since he was a teenager. I owed his old man a favor and got him hired as an officer, and he's a damn good officer too. When I put my retirement paperwork in, it was Preston I requested as my replacement. The town council votes on who the township hires as Chief of Police. It was between you and Preston. I backed Preston and used up my last favors trying to get him selected.

"In the end, even my favors weren't enough to get Preston selected as Chief. The council voted five to zero to hire you. It was a referendum on the end of my career here in Cape May. The council wanted to move in a different direction, away from anyone or anything bearing my name." Browning said.

"So, there could be a motive then?" McNamara said.

"How do you figure?"

"If Preston was denied the job of Chief of Police, he could have hatched a revenge plot against the township for not hiring him. A way to get back at Cape May and besmirch the township by concocting this Grim Reaper character with the murders." McNamara suggested.

"Unlikely," Browning replied, driving past the first checkpoint compromised of the Cape May Police department. The Cape May Sheriff's Office was set up at the opposite end of the street.

"Call it convenient, but I don't believe for one second an anonymous source directly calls a police detective with information about a white van we are looking for. The white van was information which wasn't released to the media. I also don't believe Preston forgot to close the garage door and let that van hang out if he was the killer." Browning countered.

Arriving at the Cape May Sheriff's blockade, Browning pulled the Ford Interceptor off to the side, and as he exited the vehicle, detectives Brown and Mattias met him.

"Any updates?" Browning asked.

"The Sheriff's Office liaison in this matter is Delgado. Out of courtesy to you and the sensitive nature of who the suspect is, Delgado wanted to speak with you prior to conducting the raid." Detective Brown said as the four men walked to the operational trailer where the head of the Cape May Sheriff's Office operation, Marcus Delgado, coordinated with two men dressed in black tactical gear. When he was finished issuing orders, he turned to address Browning.

"Chief Browning, Marcus Delgado, Sheriff's Office," Delgado said, shaking Browning's hand. "I appreciate the confidence you have in letting us run this operation. We have cameras trained on the outside front door of Preston's home. So far, there hasn't been any movement. We have two tactical teams preparing to breach the household using flashbangs."

"He won't use that door. There is a side door with brick steps near the driveway. He uses that entrance." Browning said pointing at the video screen.

Browning had never met Delgado before this meeting. Protocol dictated that once a warranted search or raid of a suspect's residence began, the controlling authority rested with that department. In the case of Preston's residence, that meant the Sheriff's Office. Browning had the dilemma of wanting to be the one to interview William Preston but also avoid his department conducting the raid.

"Lieutenant Delgado, Preston has friends in the Cape May Township Police Department. It will only be a matter of time before someone leaks information and picks up the phone, warning Preston we are out here, so time is of the essence in this operation. If your team enters the home, Preston, armed with his service weapon, may begin shooting. What if there was a way to ensure he is unarmed when your team breaches the door?"

"I'm open to suggestions. What are you thinking, Browning?"

"Chief McNamara and I approach the side door, and we ring the bell. Wake him up. Preston looks out the window sees only us then answers the door unarmed. We ask him why he isn't answering his phone during a police emergency. Preston will say we never called, and we'll play dumb and ask him to get his cell phone to double-check. You send the team inside to get him when he walks away from the front door. He'll be right there, unarmed."

"I'd be putting your lives into potential danger," Delgado said.

"There's no danger. Preston doesn't know he's a suspect. A lot happened last night. We could be there for a lot of reasons."

"Ok. Preston's your boy, so it's your call. But if I get the slightest vibe, something is going to happen; my guys are going in hot and taking him into custody."

"Not a problem, Lieutenant. I appreciate your assistance in this matter." Browning said as he turned around and took the two steps down off the tactical trailer.

Outside the trailer, detectives Mattias and Brown were leaning on the nearest Sheriff's Office SUV, drinking cups of coffee. Both men stood up straight, aware of their supervisors' approach, as Browning walked towards them.

"Ok. This is our play. Brown, I need you to go back to where our officers have the streets blocked off with their squad cars. Pull your car up on the sidewalk, make sure you have a visual of Preston's house, and wait for my signal to pull up to the house. Make sure to keep the car running and ready to go." Browning said, reaching into the front leather cuff case of Mattias belt and retrieving a pair of silver handcuffs. Browning then placed the cuffs into the side pocket of his jacket. Brown turned, coffee cup in hand, and began speed walking towards the blocked-off street where the nearest township Police Department vehicle was located.

"Mathias, I want you to stay with Lieutenant Delgado in that trailer. More to the point, I need thirty or forty seconds of interference. Don't get physical with him but impede his departure from the trailer for as long as possible. You know, stand in the doorway when he tries to leave." Browning said, taking Mattias's cup of coffee out of his hand.

"No problem," Mattias said, wandering to the tactical trailer.

Turning away, Browning and McNamara started the walk across the vacant street. Neighbors in windows from the adjacent houses were pulling their blinds and curtains back, looking at the two men in uniform walking across the street.

"So, what's the plan?" McNamara said.

"Here, take these. Have them ready to slap on Preston when his back is towards you," Browning said, removing the handcuffs from his pocket and handing them to McNamara. "Keep the cuffs out of site. If Delgado sees them in his camera, he may think something is up."

Browning stepped up on the curb in front of the red brick single-story home belonging to Preston and removed the lid from the cup of coffee he had stolen from Mattias. The steam from the warmth of the liquid rose out of the cup, indicating its hot contents.

From the corner of his eyes, McNamara could see two five-person teams in body armor begin moving up the street, staying out of sight from the house's windows. The team members from the Sheriff's Department blended their bodies with the shrubbery and short plastic fences surrounding the property.

"Stand on the bottom step. We want to block Preston's vision to the street and keep your hands in your pockets. We want to appear non-threatening. When Preston's back turns to you, come up the second step quick, grab the arm nearest to you, and slap the cuffs on him. I'll pin the other arm behind him."

The stairs leading to the side door of Preston's house were also made of the same red brick with a painted white metal frame handrail. The outer door had a screen window and then a wooden door behind it. McNamara stood at the bottom of the first step while Browning vaulted up the second and third steps, opened the screen door, and began banging on the wooden door. Repeating the rapping every few seconds.

Behind him, McNamara saw a window blind pulled down inside and then released back into place. He saw that Preston was looking to see who was at the door before going to answer. Despite the look out the window, Browning increased the furious rate of knocking to a rapid pounding on the door, indicating urgency. Then the door opened, and William Preston was standing there with no shoes, wearing a black Metallica T-shirt and blue jeans.

"Chief Browning? What's going on? Why all the commotion?" Preston asked, wiping sleep from his eyes. Browning stepped back from the door and down to the next step allowing the screen door to close.

"Preston, thank God you are alright. We were worried about you. We received information the lunatic may be hunting down Cape May Police Officers after last night at the church." Browning lied.

"Hunting Police Officers? No, Chief, everything is ok here. Why didn't you just call me."

"We needed to complete visual checks on all the officers who didn't answer their phones. You were next on our list to check on." Browning said, continuing his lie.

"I appreciate you and Chief McNamara checking on me," Preston said from behind the screen door.

"Ok, we have a few officers left to check on. Well, I'm sorry about the damage to your front porch."

"Damage to my front porch. What are you talking about? There's no damage to my front porch." Preston objected.

"A whole column is missing, steps too. I thought maybe you were fixing the porch up, but maybe a car took them out instead. I'm surprised you didn't see it when you came home this morning. That amount of damage would be kind of hard to miss." Browning goaded, turning his back to Preston.

Preston slammed open the screen door and placed his bare feet on the red brick staircase. Browning turned around and leaned towards Preston spilling the still warm coffee on Preston's Metallica shirt and pants.

"Ahhh. Watch it with that coffee." Preston yelped, focusing on the hot coffee spilled on him and not worrying about the damage to his porch. While looking at his soiled shirt and pants, Preston exposed his back to McNamara, who slipped up the two steps and grabbed Preston's nearest wrist. Torquing Preston's elbow to a ninety-degree angle and pinning the wrist at an uncomfortable angle, Preston leaned against the white railing. In contrast, Browning grabbed the opposite arm and struggled to pin it behind Preston's back. The cuff bracelets clicked together, and Preston began objecting.

"What is going on here? Chief Browning, let me go." Preston argued, still struggling while being led off the steps to the front of the driveway. The Cape May Sheriff's office swat teams swarmed from both sides toward the house. Reaching the end of the driveway, Browning looked up at the end of the street, lifted up his arm, and signaled with his index and middle finger for Brown to drive the car up.

Lieutenant Delgado and his team members from the tactical trailer were rounding the corner as the patrol car stopped in front of the two Police Chiefs and their prisoner. McNamara began reading Preston his Miranda rights as Browning opened the patrol car's back door, pushed Preston's head down, and placed him in the back seat.

"Get out, Brown. McNamara, and I will escort Preston down to the station. Stay here and help execute the search warrant. I want the van processed for evidence." Browning ordered as Brown exited the vehicle.

Before getting into the car from both sides, Browning could hear Lieutenant Delgado yelling for Browning to stop. Delgado ran toward the squad car, trying to prevent them from leaving the scene.

Browning lifted his right hand in the air and flipped Delgado the middle finger before driving off.

"That will go over really well with inter-departmental relations," McNamara said, getting into the patrol car on the opposite side.

"You really think I was going to turn over one of my officers to another agency. No, this is an internal matter. The Cape May Police Department will handle this. Besides, Delgado is a dick; anyone could see that. Standing in that trailer with his high-tech cameras and body armor." Browning mocked. "I accomplished with a cup of coffee what twenty of his men couldn't do back there. I arrested the suspect without any loss of property or life."

"This lack of cooperation between departments wouldn't have anything to do with the fact that two of your friends are dead?" McNamara asked.

"This is our investigation. Who the victims are is beside the point. Allowing the Sheriff's Office to get intertwined with this investigation would only cut our investigation off at the knees. Receiving and giving information would be fucked. Vital clues would be missed or overlooked." Browning snorted.

"You know the FBI called this morning wanting to send a profiler to assist us on this case," McNamara said.

"Fuck the FBI. Fuck the Sheriff's Office, and fuck you too, McNamara, if you can't see this. This is our case. We have leads; we can handle this investigation. We are getting close." Browning said.

"At what expense? How many more deaths are we willing to accept? How many relationships with other departments will we allow to burn in your pursuit of this Grim Reaper?" McNamara asked.

"As many as it takes," Browning said, looking in the rearview mirror at Preston.

October 27, 2022
Friday 2:14pm

Browning exited the interview room where McNamara was lingering outside.

"Has he given you anything?" McNamara asked, handing Browning a plastic cup of fountain water.

"No. Preston swears he didn't know anything about the van or the murders. He says the van wasn't there when he came home from work this morning. Worse, he has an alibi for the time of the death when Reverend Mulvaney was murdered. He was at work on patrol on the overnight shift." Browning said, taking a sip of the water. "What about Brown and Mattias? Have they been in touch?"

"Yes. Brown called in about twenty minutes ago. To start with, Delgado is beyond pissed, pulling all of his team out of Preston's house, and saying he'll be speaking with the Attorney General for the State of New Jersey to see about filing an ethics complaint against the department, me, and you. Delgado's also been in touch with the mayor's office, who also asked that you give him a call." McNamara answered.

"The mayor's a bozo who's been out for my head since he got elected. Ethics complaints can be really scary, except they take years to resolve. What about the crime scene at Preston's house?"

"The steering wheel, door handles, and console of the white van recovered at Preston's house returned negative results for any fingerprints. The keys were left in the ignition. They were wiped clean and or the suspect wore gloves the whole time. Forensics is taking the van for a deeper inspection looking for trace evidence or fibers. There were no license plates recovered on the van either but using the registration on the inside panel of the door reveals it was stolen four months ago in Pennsylvania."

"Did the search of Preston's home turn up anything?" Browning asked.

"A preliminary search of the residence reveals nothing incriminating, two firearms both legally registered. Preston's computer and cell phone are both being sent to the crime laboratory for search history results. But, besides the van being at the location, we don't have much. Oh, there was a preliminary toxicology report from Gil Epson's autopsy, the drug in question is Scopolamine, otherwise known in the United States as Devil's Breath. Renders the victim conscious but immobile. Basically, an organic-based liquid date rape drug."

"Any idea how rare this Devil's Breath is or where it can be obtained from?" Browning asked.

"Another dead end, it is stored at every university, medical school, and hospital around the county. In effect, we just grew our suspect list to include millions of people." McNamara sighed.

"What about the number of the anonymous phone that tipped Brown off? Is there a chance we could trace that call and identify who tipped us off?"

"I was busy with that while you were interviewing Preston. The call came in as a blocked number. I contacted the phone company, who was able to retrieve the number. We were able to trace the number back to a throw-away phone, a burner phone. The phone company is attempting to place a tracer and ping its location. We'll get an approximate location if it should be turned on and used again." McNamara answered.

"Looks like we are back to square one again with very few leads and no real suspects," Browning said, running the palm of his hand through his thick black-grey hair.

"Not entirely. This is just my two cents, but if I were you, I would reach out to your remaining friends in that picture hanging at Biaggi's pizzeria and see if they have noticed anything suspicious. Maybe they made some enemies during their tenure on the town council. Maybe one of them knows something?" McNamara suggested.

"I'll take it under advisement. In the meantime, transfer Preston to protective custody in the county jail. We'll hold him forty-eight hours or until his attorneys become obnoxious enough that we are forced to discharge him." Browning said.

"I always thought we needed to charge an individual with a crime to hold them against their will?" McNamara responded.

"Now's not the time to get cute with me, McNamara. Just do what I am asking you to do." Browning ordered.

"Alright, fine, but you are signing the transfer and detaining paperwork. When Preston sues the department, it's you his attorney can reach out for in Florida." McNamara said.

"I'll sign the paperwork, but I want you and Mathias to personally take him to the Cape May County jail. Please see that Preston gets there. Remember, don't mix him in with the general population inmates." Browning reiterated.

"You do know once I get Preston in the back of the car, someone is going to tip off the press, and that officer's picture will be all over tonight's news cast and the internet. It won't matter if he's innocent or guilty. People will see his picture and associate him forever with the Grim Reaper murders. Look what happened to Richard Jewell in ninety-six when he saved those people from being blown up in Atlanta during the Olympics. The FBI talked to Jewell a few times, and he was martyred by the media forever as the person who planted the explosives." McNamara said, trying to talk Browning out of this course of action.

"Chief McNamara, up to this point, your assistance, in this case, has been commendable, but technically you aren't supposed to start until next month. If you wish to continue with your role in this investigation, I suggest you follow orders when they are given." Browning said, pulling rank.

"Yes, Chief, as you say, I'll have the paperwork prepared for your signature and will assist in escorting Preston to the County jail. Then with your permission, I'm calling it a day and getting some sleep if you don't mind, sir," McNamara said after a brief period of silence before turning and walking away.

Browning stood at the water tank in the hallway, cursing under his breath as McNamara walked away. He knew that under a standard investigation detaining a suspect without charging them for longer than necessary was a major civil rights violation. Something has to turn up soon, some type of evidence, maybe something he was missing which could point to the identity of the Grim Reaper. At that moment, the words of Linda Martin came playing back into his mind. She didn't believe in coincidences, and suddenly, Browning didn't either.

Walking past his secretary Carrie Stewart's desk, she attempted to stop him and hand him a stack of post-it notes.

"The phones won't stop ringing, from the mayor, the Commissioner for the Sheriff's Office to internal affairs and the news media all asking for statements. I collated these notes in order of priority, starting with the mayor." Carrie explained as she handed the stack of three-by-three square notes to Browning, who didn't stop and continued to his office.

"Carrie, unplug your phone for the rest of the afternoon if anyone should get through the phone lines to you for me. I'm out of the office." Browning huffed, slamming his door.

Sitting behind his large maple dark brown desk, Browning shifted through the notes. At another time, another place, his asshole would have puckered up seeing the phone messages, some repeating three or four times. Browning tossed the post-it notes into the trash can beside his desk and removed his cell phone from his jacket pocket. The phone was turned off. Earlier in the day, simply having the phone set to vibrate was becoming a distraction, so Browning felt the need to turn the phone off for a few hours.

After powering his phone on, the icon for voice mail messages and text messages anchored to the top left of his screen came on. Deciding he could go through those messages and texts later, Browning hit the dialer icon and scrolling through the first few names in his contact list, came across the name of Morris Armstrong.

Armstrong was the fifth member of the town council in the nineteen nineties through two thousand and six. Armstrong had been the jack of all trades, dealing in real estate, and was part owner of the Cape May County Herald newspaper. Before Google and the internet, local news was still distributed by print; if influence or smear needed to be accomplished, well-timed articles in the Cape May County Herald were necessary.

The five members of the council-controlled and influenced every part of Cape May. Browning through police enforcement, Biaggi with control over the shop and retail owners, Reverend Mulvaney with the Church, and its parishioners. Boats, fish, and seafood would not move from their respective docks without input from Gilbert Epson. Still, the most critical part of the council's power was control over news articles swaying readers to form an opinion that would benefit the council members.

Browning decided his sole option remaining was to take the advice of McNamara and begin calling the two other remaining council members who were still alive. Pressing on Armstrong's name in the cell phone rolodex, the cell phone began to ring, and Browning brought the receiver closer to his ear. On the sixth ring, the phone went to voice mail.

"Sorry I missed your call. Please leave me your name and a brief message, and I'll be sure to get back to you. Bye." Morris Armstrong's voice said on the recording.

"Morris, it's Clyde, Clyde Browning. I need you to call me when you get this. It's important. I'll speak to you later." Browning said, pressing the hang-up button on the screen.

The second number Browning pressed was for Biaggi's Restaurant. After pressing the button, the phone was answered on the second ring, and a familiar voice answered.

"Biaggi's pizza. May I take your order, please?" Antonio Biaggi asked.

"Tony, it's Clyde. Can I speak with you privately if you have a minute?" Browning replied.

"Sure, let me hang up and call you from the back office," Biaggi said, hanging up the phone, and Browning was left staring at the blank screen for what felt like an eternity, but it was less than a minute when his phone rang.

"Clyde?" Biaggi's thick Italian voice said at the other end of the phone when Clyde answered.

"Tony, have you heard about Mulvaney?" Browning asked.

"It's been on the news all day that you have a suspect in custody. Is that true?" Biaggi asked. The old Italian sounded worried over the phone,

Browning thought. In all his years on the council, Biaggi was always the toughest of the five of them.

"The suspect's a plant, a red herring. The Grim Reaper put us on him to throw us off his trail. Listen, I have a question for you. Is there anything you can think of during our time sitting on the council as to why someone may want to retaliate against us?" Browning asked.

"Clyde, you know we buried many people politically during our tenure. Took advantage of several hundred more at least. But we both know the major reason I don't sleep well at night, even after all these years, is about the thing we did with the missing girl and a certain pedophile shop owner." Biaggi answered.

"That's been forefront on my mind as the most likely candidate for motive as well. Especially since Jennifer Martin showed back up a few days ago." Browning echoed.

"It's funny you say that; Jennifer Martin was here yesterday getting very friendly with a certain doctor."

"You mean Jennifer Martin was with McDonough. Doctor Bryan McDonough at your pizza place yesterday?" Browning asked.

"Yes. They took a few slices and sat outside next to one another, and their backs were turned toward me, and I am guessing they didn't think anyone would notice. But from the shop window, I saw Jennifer Martin holding Dr. McDonough's hand. It was brief, but I noticed." Biaggi said.

"Sonna of a bitch. I'll have a talk with our friend, the doctor, later. One last thing, when was the last time you spoke to Morris?" Browning solicited.

"Not in a day or so. Any reason to be concerned?" Biaggi answered.

"I tried him on his cell phone, and he didn't answer. For someone in real estate to not answer their phone is always concerning. Do me a favor, Antonio, and watch your back. This Grim Reaper has killed two of us; there stands a chance he could come for the rest of us." Browning said.

"I'm carrying my protection with me at all times now, fully loaded with sixteen rounds," Biaggi said, hanging up the phone. He sounded like the typical Italian mobster saying those last words, sixteen rounds, Browning thought, putting his cell phone away.

Looking at the cell phone, he had over twenty-five voice mails and another forty or so texts all since this morning. Returning these messages would take hours, and most were from people Browning was trying to avoid. Therefore, they could wait.

Browning sat back in his chair and thought about Dr. McDonough and Jennifer Martin holding hands outside the pizzeria. It was a little too convenient for McDonough to show up and do pro-bono work, therefore inserting himself into this case.

Would Dr. McDonough have access to the Devil's Breath? Browning's gut told him yes. Perhaps a talk with McDonough would shed some light on his involvement. But first, Browning needed to conduct a house call.

October 27, 2022

Friday 4:45pm

The drive from six four three Washington Street to Foster Ave took Browning less than ten minutes with traffic and the occasional streetlight. Browning seized the time in the Ford Explorer to redial Morris Armstrong's number another three times, letting the cell phone ring on each call until it was answered by Morris's voice mail. Browning had never known Armstrong not to pick up his cell phone, let alone not answer four calls in a row. The intrepid feeling he was heading toward danger crept up Browning's back in a sweat chill, causing him to perspire through the middle of the back of his pressed shirt.

Instead of being nervous, Browning felt energized. Driven with determination to end the

Grim Reaper murderer as he drove toward Morris Armstrong's residence. For the first time in a long while, Browning found himself feeling more alive than at time during the last few years, fueled with purpose. The endorphins were kicking in creating a natural high.

Armstrong's house on Foster was located on an expensive piece of real estate with a view overlooking the Cape May Canal. The three-bedroom, two-bath with attached garage and stained brown front porch complete with rocking chairs appeared undisturbed with the cloudy grey backdrop in the sky overhead. The wind velocity increased indicating that night was approaching soon and maybe an early winter as well. Parking in the driveway, Browning unbuttoned his heavy jacket and removed his police issue forty-five from its holster, taking the safety off and racking the slide.

He had only fired the weapon once in all his years on the police force, killing Evan Peterson, the owner of the ice cream parlor who had abducted Jennifer Martin. The irony of these two cases removed several years apart from one another being related was not lost on Browning as he exited the Explorer.

Walking toward the garage, Browning stood on his tip toes and peered in through the garage window catching a glimpse of Armstrong's black BMW. Morris didn't own any other cars. Browning thought Armstrong was most likely home as he took the two steps up the stained wooden porch and knocked on the front door. With no answer, Browning knocked on the door a second time, then went to the large living room bay window with its curtains pulled back.

Cupping his hand over his eyes, Browning peered into the living room. The lack of light from the outside, mixed with the shadows inside, made it difficult to see. Giving his eyes some time to adjust to the darkness of the living room, Browning could make out the living room furniture was in disarray. Extending his vision in the dark to the back wall, crouched in the living room was the white glow of a naked man bound at his wrists and ankles. His mouth was stuffed with a white cloth to prevent him from screaming. The man's head stuck out of a wood box, preventing him from moving.

To the side of the bound Morris Armstrong, a shadowed silhouette in the darkness was standing over him. An all-black figure dressed in a robe, holding a scythe. Browning could make out the distinguishable skeleton mask of the Grim Reaper standing in the shadows towering over Armstrong. Then the unexpected occurred, Morris Armstrong was moving, wiggling back and forth in the wooden holding device while muffled sounds came from his gagged mouth.

"Hold on, Morris, I'm coming." Browning thought, removing the forty-five from its holster and making his way to the front door. "I got the drop on him if he didn't see me, so shoot first." Browning thought, sizing up the front door as he measured the doorknob and kicked the inseam open. The door splintered apart, and Browning took two quick steps in the entryway, firing four shots at the unmoving Grim Reaper standing over Armstrong.

A succession of events occurred as the bullets struck their mark. Three popping sounds and a release of a gas-like hissing sound as the black robe began swaying back and forth and then lifting toward the ceiling. A whooshing cord swam past Browning on the wall to his right and then lifted toward the ceiling, releasing a painted black blade onto the back of Morris Armstrong's neck, separating his head from his body with a violent thump.

Blood began to spew in a violent cascade of dark red onto the wall as Morris Armstrong's head separated from his body. The guillotine blade and Armstrong's body fell onto the floor, discharging dark black blood onto the carpeting. His mouth was still gagged as his separated head rolled several feet on the ground and landed sideways, his eyes still wide open, focused on Browning as Armstrong's brain processed its last bit of information. Still attempting to process what had occurred moments before, Browning turned and threw up on the entryway patio where he had kicked in the door.

Wiping the puke from the sides of his mouth with the sleeve of his jacket, Browning moved back to the living room wall and flipped on the light switch, turning on the recessed lights embedded overhead. The crime scene was now illuminated. The black liquid which had spewed from the bound corpse of Morris Armstrong was now a dark red. The whites of Armstrong's eyes were fixed in a cock-eyed angle, looking straight up at the ceiling. Stepping over the separated head, Browning moved to the floating dark cloak figure of the Grim Reaper and found underneath a white laundry bag filled with helium balloons. The scythe was a plastic blow up and behind the skull's bone white mask was a larger balloon with Happy Halloween inscribed on its front.

Browning let the Grim Reaper mask slip from his hand and fall to the bloodied floor before reaching into his pocket and getting his cell phone to dial nine-one-one.

***

Browning sat outside the crime scene in the white rocking chair, rocking back and forth while the Medical Examiner's Office and detectives Brown and Mathias processed the crime scene inside. Browning was oblivious to the goings on around him and behind him. His forty-five, now used in an officer-related shooting, was taken as evidence.

As he rocked back and forth in the chair on Armstrong's porch, he took his fingernail and slowly peeled the chipped white paint away from the armrest exposing the light brown sanded wood underneath.

"Did you hear me?" Chief McNamara repeated.

"What? I'm sorry, I wasn't listening." Browning said, coming out of his daze.

"Are you alright? I can't imagine what you must be going through seeing your friend beheaded inside." McNamara sympathized, placing his hand on Browning's shoulder as a sign of condolence and taking a seat in the chair next to him.

"You were right all along. I tried to deny it. I didn't want to admit it. In some way, the council is connected to these murders from years ago. I came to Morris' house because deep down, I knew you were right." Browning said, staring straight ahead into the distance.

"Don't beat yourself up. This Grim Reaper is beating us all and making the whole department look bad." McNamara said. "Now, for some unpleasant news, the mayor and the Town Council issued a referendum after the stunt you pulled with Officer Preston. They wanted you out of the office effective today. I spoke some sense into them and talked about the Halloween parade and the safety of the children for tomorrow's event. I told them no one knows the plans for the parade better than you. They consented to you being there in an advisory capacity only and will let you resign first thing Monday morning."

"He'll strike tomorrow at the parade. All of these murders so far have been grandiose, almost as if he's on a stage. Tomorrow during the parade, it's the biggest stage of the year." Browning commented.

"I pray you are wrong," McNamara said as detective Mathias came out onto the porch.

"Chief Browning, Chief McNamara. I have the preliminary results from the crime scene inside. I wouldn't beat yourself up about the homicide of Morris Armstrong too much, Chief, the wooden device that decapitated Armstrong was a makeshift Guillotine.

"You couldn't see the blade from the outside because it had been spray-painted black. Without seeing the reflection of the steel blade from the outside, there was no way for you to know. Your entry into the house via the front door triggered a trap of fishing lines that held the blade over Armstrong's head. We found the same fishing wires tied to the back door. Entry through either door and swoosh, the fishing lines were cut, and the blade would fall, beheading Armstrong.

"The trap would have been impossible to see from the outside based on the thinness of the wires. The blade itself may be thirty or forty pounds. Nothing a few well-placed fishing lines couldn't hold in place.

"As for the balloon figure of the Grim Reaper; underneath the cloak was a laundry bag filled with helium balloons, making it appear from the outside that you saw a figure clad in a black cloak standing over the victim. You can buy the cloak, plastic scythe, balloons, and mask at any party store in New Jersey this time of year or on the internet. Brown and I will start making inquiries at the local shops and extend our search to the surrounding towns to see if we turn anything up. We'll also run the cloak for fiber and hair and try and dust the balloons for fingerprints." Detective Mathias reported to the two men sitting on the porch.

"Anything else, detective?" Chief McNamara asked.

"One other thing, the Medical Examiner believes he found two puncture marks similar to the ones found on the previous victims near what remains of Armstrong's neck, indicating he was most likely doped up in order to be subdued," Mathias added.

"Thank you, detective. That will be all." Chief McNamara said, and when Mathias had gone back inside, McNamara returned his attention to Browning. "Under the circumstances, I believe it would be best to place you and Anthony Biaggi under protective custody, at least until Monday, when you resign."

"I already spoke with Biaggi. He won't have protective custody. He did send his wife to her sister's house just out of caution." Browning said.

"We should at least assign a car outside Biaggi's house for the night, but with the parade tomorrow, we can't afford the officers to sit on him during the day," McNamara suggested.

"Make the call for tonight. Have an officer sit outside his house. With the parade tomorrow, Biaggi will be safe inside his pizzeria. It's the busiest day of the non-summer months for him." Browning said.

"What about you? Do you want to enter into protective custody? I can make the arrangements." McNamara asked.

"No. I'll be surrounded by people and police during the parade tomorrow." Browning said.

"What about tonight?" McNamara replied.

"I have another gun or two at home for protection. If the Reaper tries anything, I'll kill him." Browning stated.

"Fair Enough. Go home and try and get some sleep, Clyde, and I'll see you tomorrow." McNamara responded.

October 27, 2022
Friday 7:15pm

The day light grew shorter, and the remaining sun in the sky was already gone, disappearing over the trees and houses as an orange tinge illuminating the grey sky above separated the earth and clouds. Browning drove his personal vehicle on a side street adjacent to Washington Square and Franklin Street. Before parking his car on the side street near the Washington Square Mall and with a clear view of the post office, Browning sat staking out the long lines of Victorian Bed Breakfasts lining Franklin towards the sea.

Exiting his vehicle, Browning placed a black ski hat on his head and zipped his thin black windbreaker up to his collar to obscure his face. Concealing his appearance would not draw any unusual attention as the steady October winds made most passers-by bundle up for warmth and cast their gaze and heads down away from the October winds. Walking the two blocks down Washington and turning onto Madison, Browning stopped across the street from the house he came to observe.

The lights were still out, and the man he considered his prime suspect for the Grim Reaper murders was still not home. Keeping his hands in his pockets as he crossed Madison Street, Browning walked past the open blue painted iron grated fence and up the driveway of the two-story wood-shingled home. While most of the houses in Cape May were undergoing renovations or updates, this home was still antiquated, and not been refurnished since circa nineteen forty-four.

A motion detector spotlight illuminated his presence in the backyard, and Browning stopped and froze, aware he was visible standing in the neighbor's backyard. The houses on both sides of the two-story brown shingled house, like all properties near the Washington Square Mall and Bed and Breakfast district, sat on top of one another.

Browning held his breath and turned his head to his right and left, seeing lights inside both homes. Kitchen and bedroom windows overlooked the backyard, but none of the residents had become aware of the stranger dressed in black walking through their neighbor's backyard.

With the motion detector light still shining overhead, Browning walked up to the backyard porch and peered inside the dark vacant house. Removing the thirty-six-ounce, fourteen-inch Maglite from inside his jacket, Browning placed the back cap of the Maglite through the window of the kitchen door. The window shattered without much resistance, and Browning pulled the black ski hat down over his face, where he had cut two holes and a third for his mouth for a make-shift ski mask. Reaching inside the broken window, Browning placed his hand on the inside door handle and unlocked the door pushing aside the layer of glass shards as he walked over the broken glass and began his search of Doctor McDonough's residence.

Doctor Bryan McDonough carrying his leather portfolio binder, walked up his front door and put his key in the top lock as he had done thousands of times since he was a boy coming home from school. Opening the door, McDonough placed his portfolio case on the round table near the entry and began fumbling in the dark, searching for the vase lamp which occupied the table. The two-story brown shingled house had not seen an electrical update; therefore, plug-in lights were still used instead of recess or chandelier lighting.

The problem was that the vase lamp on the table nearest the entryway was not where it had been for the last thirty years. In fact, the table was empty. Using the little light coming through the window from the street to guide his hand, McDonough began searching in his jacket pockets for his cell phone when he realized the door behind him had shut. Turning his body in the dark toward the closing door, he had just reached his cell phone when he was struck on the clavicle by what felt like a steel pipe by a figure lurking in the shadows.

McDonough dropped to his knees in pain. The cell phone McDonough was searching for fell from his hand into the darkness, lost on the hardwood floor. McDonough reeled in pain, trying to lift himself off the floor using only his one good arm. His shoulder was most likely broken or shattered as McDonough held himself up with his right hand. The masked intruder took the elongated steel object and struck McDonough across the forehead, causing him to see stars before he blacked out.

It was some time before McDonough awoke, sensing first the terrible throbbing in his head and then when he tried to move, feeling the pain radiate throughout his left shoulder. The pain made McDonough recall the assault, which had occurred when he walked into the darkness of his house. Attempts to move his body were met with resistance, his hands bound behind him as he was tied to a wooden chair.

His left eye was puffed closed from the strike across his face and could only be opened a fraction of the way. He was in a familiar place, but the recognition from a new viewpoint delayed his response. Seeing the shower tiles from a new angle, McDonough realized the chair he was sitting in was placed in the bathtub.

McDonough began to rock back and forth, wiggling the ropes from around his wrists, trying to break free from the chair he was tied to.

"You realize it's futile, don't you?" The voice from the opposite side of the bathroom said, pulling the shower curtain aside. It was a familiar voice, distinct, but through his headache and from the deepest recesses of his memory, McDonough could recall the name of the voice's owner.

The attacker turned on the light above the medicine cabinet; still sensitive from the blow to his head, the illumination hurt McDonough enough to close his eyes as the pounding in his head persisted.

"What do you want from me?" McDonough cried, now aware that another rope aside from the ones binding his hands was tied around his neck leading up to the metal shower head.

"I want to have a talk. An honest talk." The masked assailant answered.

"I have office hours, you know."

"I doubt you would be so forthcoming with me in an open-door setting. You see, the information I need to know is about one of your patients. Jennifer Martin."

"What about her?" McDonough shrieked, opening his injured left eye to look at the masked man speaking to him.

"I know that's not Jennifer Martin. My question is, how deeply are you involved with her?"

"I don't follow you. What makes you think that's not Jennifer Martin? I am not involved with her in any way." McDonough disputed.

"See, Doctor, I placed a rope around your neck with the other end tied to the shower head. If you continue asking questions instead of providing answers, I will kick the chair out from underneath you and break your neck. After your neck snaps, I will cut the ropes off your corpse and make it look like a suicide. I'll even write a cute little note about how you were beat up by your gay lover and couldn't stand his rejection." The assailant threatened.

"But no one would believe that. I'm not gay. I don't have a gay lover."

"Does it really matter? The world will move on without you in it. Now what I need to know is how you are involved with the Grim Reaper. The answer, please." Browning said, tilting McDonough's chair back on its two back feet tightening the cord around his neck.

"I'm not involved with the Grim Reaper; I swear to you." McDonough squealed.

"Ok. Let's try this another way. I believe the woman claiming to be Jennifer Martin is somehow involved with the Grim Reaper. Why don't you tell me about your dating history with your patient, and please be specific?" Browning asked, turning the shower on and letting the cold water run over the tied-up McDonough.

"Browning, I swear I am not sexually involved with her." McDonough pleaded as the chair rocked back and forth over the slippery bathtub floor.

"You recognized me, despite the mask? Tisk tisk, you shouldn't be so smart, Doctor. You should also know I have a witness who spotted you and your patient Jennifer Martin getting friendly and holding hands earlier today. Go ahead and deny it. I dare you." Browning gnarled his teeth at the man being soaked by the running water.

"Go downstairs and open my briefcase. I terminated my relationship with Jennifer Martin today. That's why I was late getting home. During her treatment, to help her regain her memory, I thought it would be therapeutic to drive around town and see familiar places. When we went to lunch, she repeatedly tried to hold my hand. It is not unusual for a patient to develop feelings for their therapist.

"I admit, at first, I was flattered, but I always stood my ground. The relationship between doctor and patient was too important. At the end of lunch, I told her I could no longer be her doctor or see her. I referred her to a female colleague. I swear, check my briefcase." McDonough screamed.

Browning turned the water off overhead and stopped rocking the chair back and forth.

"I believe you are telling the truth, but that's not Jennifer Martin. There's no way that's Jennifer Martin. She's playing you, doc. She's played all of us."

"I shouldn't tell you this. It violates patient-client confidentiality. We made progress today with Jennifer's memory. When we drove past her childhood house, her mom's house now, she recalled a memory from her childhood." McDonough said.

"Go on. I'm listening." Browning said, tilting the chair back slightly once again so McDonough could feel the cord wrapped round his neck.

"She recalled playing outside with her friends and a police officer showing up and going inside the house to meet with her mother. She identified you as the officer visiting her house. Her memory was of you Browning visiting her mother when she was a child."

Browning let go of the tilted chair, and the chair fell forward on all four legs, and McDonough let out a loud breath of air as if he had escaped execution at the last moment. Browning stood in the bathroom, thinking. He knew there was no possible way at all he could be wrong about the past regarding the truth surrounding Jennifer Martin.

But there was no one else but Jennifer Martin, who knew about his past relationship with her mother, Linda Martin. Not even Linda's ex-husband knew they were together. The cogs inside Browning's mind were churning, but he needed more time to think.

"What are you going to do with me?" McDonough sobbed.

"I need to ensure you are not involved with the Grim Reaper. If I am right, from a psychological standpoint, everything the Reaper has done so far has been done on a grand scale. The burning cross, the guillotine, and even the first murder in the trunk was carried out in such a way as to draw attention to the inadequacies of the Cape May Police Department, more specifically to humiliate me. So, if I am correct, there is no bigger opportunity for the Reaper to be on the grand stage with a whole audience present than during the Halloween parade tomorrow." Browning conjectured.

"What does that have to do with me?"

"It means I will need to stash you somewhere until the parade's over. If you stay tied up until after the parade, then you really aren't involved. Believe me, I am not a murderer or a criminal, but some lunatic dressed as the Grim Reaper has killed my old friends and is coming after me. No matter what happened tonight, I had my reasons." Browning asserted, removing the rope from around McDonough's neck.

"You assaulted me, and you are going to leave me locked up." McDonough objected.

"I have no choice. I'll send someone over to do a welfare check on you tomorrow. Make sure you make a lot of noise when they get here."

"You expect me to remain quiet about you interrogating me?"

"I don't do innuendos, and I don't make threats I can't keep. You experienced first-hand the lengths I will go through to protect myself. Stay quiet until tomorrow afternoon, and when you are found, the description of your assailant better not resemble yours truly." Browning urged, tilting the chair back once more and turning the shower on overhead.

October 28, 2022

Saturday 7:55am

Biaggi had not slept well the previous night. He was preparing for the inevitable conclusion he knew was approaching, his meeting with the Grim Reaper killer. So far, his friend Chief Browning had done little to reassure him of a successful capture of the Reaper as the former Cape May council members were being picked off one at a time.

Despite this being the busiest weekend of the non-summer months, he sent his wife to his sisters for the remainder of the weekend. While he hated losing his wife when he needed her to help the most at the restaurant, Biaggi would not allow her to be used like a pawn against him. Biaggi tossed and turned in his bed, frequently checking the windows and locks while looking out the window at the police car sitting outside his house. Every time Biaggi pulled back the blinds, the police officer was busy reading a novel or playing on his cell phone instead of paying attention. Not much in the way of security, Biaggi thought as he gripped the nine-millimeter semi-automatic pistol in his hand as he moved around his house.

Even when he tried to fall asleep, Biaggi thought about all the people in the past he had taken advantage of and had screwed in business dealings who remained in Cape May or the tri-state area when he sat as the council president. There weren't many people left who would have the stamina or hate to come after not just him but the entire council after all this time.

Did anything he had done merit being executed? Sure, people were wiped out financially, and others were forced out of the area, but no one was hurt physically. To come after them all now. Over thirty years later was something else, something more serious. Biaggi tossed and turned, struggling to sleep while holding the pistol in his hand as he listened to the wind blow against the house's windows.

In the morning, Biaggi got an early start. Browning told him the day before that the unofficial police escort from overnight would stop as all officers were being put on crowd control for the upcoming Halloween parade. Parking his red corvette parallel to the building located behind his store in the alleyway behind the pizzeria, the policeman in the patrol car waved as he drove away to end his shift. Biaggi gestured back while holding the keys to the back of the pizzeria's metal door in his hand. Tucked inside his waistband was the nine-millimeter handgun.

Inserting his key into the lock of the solid rusted door, Biaggi caught a glimpse of a figure dressed in black walking his way through the alleyway. The Reaper, Biaggi thought to himself, he's come for me, but I am prepared. It had seemed to Biaggi the Reaper had appeared out of thin air some thirty yards from the back door and walking in his direction up the alley way.

Leaving the inserted key into the lock, Biaggi placed his hand on his waistband and pulled up his t-shirt. Reaching for the nine-millimeter semi-automatic pistol before brandishing the gun and taking aim at the robed clandestine figure dressed in all black coming his way.

"You won't get me, you motherfucker!" Biaggi yelled, firing twice as bullets were thrown at the two dumpsters nearest where the Reaper was standing. The Reaper side-stepped behind the nearest dumpster and out of Biaggi's view. Biaggi regripped the stock of the nine-millimeter, taking turns to rub the sweat from his hands so they would be dry.

Slowly approaching the dumpster, the Reaper hid behind, and pointing his pistol, Antonio Biaggi rounded the corner and saw nothing but empty space. Panic set in. Had the Reaper really been there? Was his night of unrest and guilty conscious been playing pranks on his eyes? He wasn't thinking straight. In a frenzy, Biaggi began pointing the pistol in all directions of the alley as if he expected the Reaper to jump out at him like in a movie. Cautiously, Biaggi began walking backward, remaining focused on where he had seen the Reaper last. Back to where the keys were still inserted into the restaurant doorway and, taking one final look around, unlocked the bolt from the rusted steel doorway.

As Biaggi entered the restaurant, he shut the steel doorway behind him and secured the bolt at the top.

"You won't get me that easy. I'm smarter than the others." Biaggi yelled at the door.

A loud rapping series of bangs on the metal door came from outside, startling him. The pistol in his hand began shaking as he pointed the gun at the steel back door and began firing in fear. It was irrational, he thought; the door, although rusted, was solid metal. Even the bullets he was firing were not going to pass through the door.

The lack of sleep combined with the adrenaline of fear would not allow him to make sense of this until the gun's slide locked in place and the last of the shells was ejected onto the restaurant's kitchen floor. Biaggi released the magazine and reached into his back pocket for the extra magazine. As he kept his eyes on the backdoor, now riddled with bullets, he backed up into the kitchen.

He would need to call someone, the police. He was inside; he was safe inside the restaurant. Outside was the threat; outside was the Reaper. How many people could say they say they looked into the face of death and lived? He wondered.

There were two phones in the restaurant, one in the manager's office and a second phone at the counter to take delivery orders. The second phone was through the push-open double doors behind him. He would call Browning, and Browning would come. It was an error to underestimate his adversary; when the police arrived, he could get away. Drive far away and telephone his wife. He would retire, sell the restaurant business, sell the block of buildings he owned directly across from the beach and promenade, sell his house, and travel. The Reaper could never catch him because he wouldn't know where he was going to be next.

Stepping backward at a deliberate pace toward the double doors while trying to estimate where the phone was, Biaggi kept his eyes trained on the bullet-ridden door. Biaggi was still fumbling the seventeen-round magazine into the magazine well of the nine-millimeter when he bumped into something behind him. There was a sharp prick, equivalent to a bee sting, pinging in between where his neck and shoulder met. If it hadn't been for the unmovable object he had bumped into, he would have ignored the slight jab in his shoulders radiating through his back muscles.

Biaggi's eyes grew bigger as he turned to look at what he had bumped into; standing in the center of the double doors was the Grim Reaper. Biaggi reached his left hand up where his shoulder and neck were burning and felt a plastic cylinder. Pulling the syringe out, Biaggi stared at the broken needle of the empty syringe. The room began to spin, and Biaggi began feeling light on his feet, the syringe dropped from his left hand, and as he lifted his eyes to where the Grim Reaper was standing in the doorway, his vision began to blur, and there were two suddenly two Reapers standing before him.

Biaggi raised the gun in his right hand and saw two guns in two of his hands. I'm going down, he thought. The Reaper poisoned me. The two guns became four as Biaggi's vision blurred, and he fell forward, squeezing the trigger once before falling onto his face on the red chimney color tile of the kitchen floor. The gun fell to his side before he blacked out.

***

Dennis Cuthbert arrived five minutes early to nine am at the warehouse as directed in the e-mail when he applied for the job as a driver online. The personal ad wanted a CDL driver, three hours pay for five hundred dollars. If the job was accepted, details on the job and instructions would follow. Cuthbert walked into the warehouse, and the e-mail provided detailed instructions for the flatbed truck to be driven as part of the Cape May Halloween parade. Payment would be left in the envelope taped to the steering wheel, and keys for the flatbed truck would be left in the ignition.

The instructions indicated Cuthbert was not to speak to the performance character on the back of the truck who needed to remain in the role of their character. He was instructed to get inside the flatbed truck, drive to Sunset Blvd, and join the parade on West Perry. At the intersection, he was to wait for the parade floats to go by, where his flatbed truck would join the rest in the Halloween parade toward Market Street and Washington Square. After the parade, he was to return the flatbed truck to the same warehouse and leave.

The double doors to the warehouse were ajar, and in the center of the warehouse was a red flatbed truck. Cuthbert didn't see anyone else in the warehouse and was tempted to yell out for assistance before remembering his instructions. Under no circumstances are you to speak with the performer. Cuthbert climbed up and opened the driver's side door looking at the decorated back of the flatbed. An unlit grilling fire pit was built underneath a large cast iron bull. The cast iron bull was spray painted black, and must have taken this group a large amount of effort to place it on the back of the flatbed.

It must be an advertisement for a restaurant, Cuthbert thought, ducking his head inside the truck's cab where he found the envelope taped to the steering wheel. Climbing into the driver's seat, Cuthbert took a second look around the warehouse from behind the steering wheel; there was still no one present, and he debated taking the envelope and leaving. Cuthbert pried open the envelope flap and saw five one-hundred-dollar bills. Placing the envelope inside the top pocket of his flannel long sleeve shirt, Cuthbert wondered where the performer he was supposed to meet was and how long he would need to wait.

Peering out between the warehouse doors, a hooded figure with the face of a skeleton dressed in a black robe carrying a scythe approached. The dark character seemed to float through the air and then stepped up on the driver's side of the vehicle and stared face to face directly at Cuthbert.

Dennis Cuthbert remembered the odd instructions not to speak to the performer once they were in character, but the person staring at him face to face had a macabre skull facemask which was giving him the hebbie jebbies. A sling of sweat ran down Dennis's lower back as he nodded at the Grim Reaper, staring at him before turning his head away and firing up the engine using the key left in the ignition.

When he glanced to his left, he was relieved to see the black robbed Reaper was gone and ascending to the flatbed behind him to begin work on firing up the cast iron bull. As he started driving through the wide double doors of the warehouse, Dennis Cuthbert stared into the rearview mirror, seeing the Grim Reaper actor lighting a fire underneath the bull as clouds of steam and smoke blew from the nostrils of the cast iron beast into the air.

October 28, 2022
Saturday 10:05am

The crowd was already forming down Main Street Market, stretching from the old ACME shopping center to the Congress Hall hotel across from the promenade and beach. Children dressed as Power Rangers and Vampires, mixed with adults customed as zombies, filled the market street shops for candy and gift certificates handed out by the shop owners as parents supervised through the crowded street. The restaurants and outside eating establishments would soon be overflowing with guests eager to get on a waiting list for lunch.

Browning was patrolling early, starting where the Main Street parade would run through and all of the establishments past the Ugly Mug bar and restaurant. McNamara patrolled the opposite side from starting on Franklin near the Our Lady of the Sea church. Officers on foot patrol were directing traffic as visitors from all over South Jersey flooded Cape May City looking for hard-to-find parking spots. Plainclothes detectives and officers ran parallel routes down the non-parade paths and side streets.

All in all, this was not the end of the career Browning had envisioned for himself. While he hadn't considered himself run out of town as Chief, the time remaining on his clock was ticking closer to midnight. The Grim Reaper murders, as the press had labeled them, had cast a black cloud over his career; worse, the murders seemed to be done to taunt him. Killing the town council members off one at a time made the imaginary target on his back feel heavier, and the sleepless nights and endless cups of coffee were wearing on him as he walked Market Street in a semi-circle.

The interrogation of Doctor McDonough had been productive. With the Doctor tied to the chair under threat of torture, he admitted Jennifer Martin had a memory of her youth. Browning as a patrolman visiting her home to carry on his affair with her mother.

On one of Browning's romantic summer interludes to the Martin residence, Jennifer Martin had disappeared, and Browning was there when it happened. He was involved. It wasn't just unlikely the woman pretending to be Jennifer Martin recalled his visitation; it was damn near impossible. Jennifer Martin was dead, Browning reminded himself as he wiped the sun from his brow and placed his hat back on his head. The sun felt good and warmed him from the cool breeze of autumn. But he felt the chill, remembering he was there when Jennifer Martin died. An event he had tried to block away and forget about for the last thirty years.

Browning was thinking about ghosts. He didn't believe in them and didn't have any faith in ghost stories or the people who told them. There would always be a rational explanation for a paranormal visit. Cape May was an old city, filled with its share of people carried away in storms and hurricanes. Hotels and boarding houses with greedy owners could capitalize on these atrocities by charging guests extra to stay in the room where these horrors occurred. But Browning considered himself a pragmatic and grounded individual. There were no ghosts, no paranormal visitors; everything had an explanation. He just needed to work through this mystery, through the lack of sleep and against the ticking clock that would absolve him of tomorrow's power.

Walking Market Street, avoiding the mass of customed tourists while trying to work through multiple problems in his mind, Browning decided the girl was not Jennifer Martin. But it seemed the evidence with that theory was stacking against him.

There were issues contradicting his memory, beginning with the matching DNA with her mother, Linda Martin, and now the memory Doctor McDonough relayed to him. A memory only Jennifer Martin would recall. This put Browning back to square one; either everyone was lying, or the amnesic woman was Jennifer Martin. If she was pretending to be Jennifer Martin, why was she acting?

"Browning, the parade's starting. Do you have a visual on the floats?" McNamara asked, coming through on the microphone on Browning's shoulder breaking his train of thought.

"That's affirmative," Browning answered, clicking the microphone as he spoke before climbing the wood box surrounding a tree so he could peer over the crowd and past the floats. On the opposite side of the street, Browning saw McNamara standing on an unoccupied bench, waving his arm at him. Browning returned the wave.

The flatbed trucks each carried different Halloween characters. Keeping his eyes trained on the crowd, Browning didn't take an interest in the parade until the Cape May Regional High School cheerleaders dressed in zombie makeup shook their pom-poms. The cheerleaders waved their arms and performed a coordinated dance alongside their school float. The cheerleader's float was followed by a magician in a top hat shooting bolts of candy in the air above the crowd as masses of children scoured the brick-paved street, scrambling for pieces of Tootsie Pops and Twizzlers. The follow-up float to the magician shooting the candy caught Browning unaware, a red-semi flat-bed trailer, and on the trailer bed was a sizeable cast-iron bull with steam coming through the bull's snout.

The dark-robed figure on the flat-bed trailer was stoking a fire under the bull as smoke carried into the crowd. The character raised the scythe over their head before facing the public in Browning's direction. Frozen in place, Browning thought at first the performer dressed as the Grim Reaper who was pointing at the crowd was tasteless, but the hairs on his arms spiked, and a chill went down his spine, and as his throat ran dry as he gulped. The truck came to a sudden halt in the middle of Main Street, and the Grim Reaper pointed at Browning standing up on the wooden box near the tree some forty yards from him.

"It's him. He's here." Browning said, his motion frozen as he feared he might startle the Grim Reaper while reaching for his microphone on his shoulder.

"Suspect is on the back of the red flat-bed truck in the middle of Main Street. I need officers to converge on this location." Browning emphasized releasing the microphone as he jumped down and when he looked up saw the Grim Reaper jump down from the back of the float.

"Suspect is attempting to flee. Heading South on Main Street." Browning could hear McNamara's voice come through the microphone on his shoulder.

The red truck sat idle, unmoving, in the center of the street. Browning attempted to push through the crowd of people as he shoved his way past children and parents who were still watching the parade come to its conclusion. Browning could see the driver of the flat-bed truck jump out on the opposite side of the truck. Browning reached for the microphone and clicked the handheld as he pushed his way to the roped-off intersection.

"McNamara, grab the driver of the flatbed coming your way. I'll continue pursuit of the main suspect heading south." Browning ordered, climbing over the yellow parade rope, and began running past the pizza and beach item shops to the parking lot in the rear of Market Street. Removing his pistol from the holster, Browning kept the firearm low ready pointed down at his feet. At the far end of the plaza, an officer Browning recognized appeared at the opposite end of the parking lot. The parking lot was full of cars waiting their turn to exit, with families of people moving in crowds trying to walk back to their vehicles.

Signaling to the police officer to go in the opposite direction away from him, Browning worked his way through the parking lot. Looking to where the officer was checking in between cars, the officer shrugged his shoulders. Two police cars with flashing lights pulled alongside the street, holding up the congested traffic and not allowing any other vehicles to exit the lot.

Several additional officers arrived on the scene less than three minutes after Grim Reaper jumped down from the parade float. The police task force was methodically combing through the parking lot but did not turn up anything. Browning looked up at the CCTV camera in the corner of the parking lot, which had been shattered. When the realization they lost the Grim reaper suspect began to kick in, McNamara came through on the microphone.

"Chief Browning, I was able to apprehend the suspect fleeing from the flat-bed truck. Did you apprehend the Reaper?"

"Negative. The suspect got away. I'm heading in your direction, have some of the officers sequester the vehicle. I want CSI to go over the truck, and we'll interrogate the driver at the station."

***

"His name is Dennis Cuthbert, thirty-seven years old from Manasquan, New Jersey. He says he was paid five hundred dollars to not ask questions and drive an actor on the back of the flat-bed float for the parade." Mattis said as Browning looked at Dennis Cuthbert through the one-way mirror opposite the interrogation room. Inside the interrogation room, detective Brown was still questioning Cuthbert.

"Do you believe him?" Browning asked, taking a sip of coffee from the Styrofoam cup.

"He had five hundred dollars in an envelope stuffed in his right pocket and a piece of paper, an e-mail based on a Craig's List ad. The alibi is so stupid; it almost has to be real." Detective Mattis responded.

"Then why did he run? Why did he try and run if he didn't do anything wrong?" Browning asked.

"Mr. Cuthbert stated, and I quote, 'the flatbed truck just stopped in the middle of the parade. I was trying to restart the engine when I heard someone yelling, police. When I turned and looked behind me, I saw a Police Officer coming my way. I panicked and tried to run out of the truck before being tackled by Chief McNamara.' End statement." Mattis said.

"So, he says. What about the truck?"

"Crime scene is still processing. The driver's claim is substantiated...slightly, there was a rigged engine cutoff switch in the rear by the bull on the trailer." Mattis said as McNamara entered the room.

"And the body, it's been identified as Antonio?" Browning asked.

"Not officially identified, no. The body was placed in the oversized cooking pot shaped like a large bull. The fire below the pot slowly roasted the victim, boiling him alive. The victim's skin and innards melted like a slow roast. When the crime scene tried to remove him from the bull, he was stuck to the pot's side. His skin peeled off, turning the victim into a stew. But a check of the pizza place reveals Mr. Biaggi is missing, sir."

"So, you are telling me this Dennis Cuthbert was driving around for two or more hours cooking a person in a large pot in the back of a truck belonging to a person he never met before, and he didn't think twice about it?" Browning asked.

"That about sums it up, sir," Mattis said.

"Hold the suspect and charge him with murder. Let the prosecutor decide if there's enough there." Browning said.

"Yes, sir," Mattis said, leaving as McNamara watched the interrogation's conclusion.

"I just got off the phone with the mayor. He wants your resignation effective immediately. The town council and the mayor are all pissed. The news outlets and media have turned our annual Halloween parade into a circus. We are already the lead story on every new outlet and internet media website. Our only saving grace is that we apprehended a suspect at the crime scene. On top of that, someone leaked photos of Biaggi cooking in that Bull-shaped pot to the Post." McNamara stated.

"Any leads on the Grim Reaper? Cameras or witnesses?" Browning asked.

"Did you not hear what I said. It's over. Your being here is over. Your friends are all gone. I used my first and last card, keeping you on for the logistics of the parade, and that blew up in my face. I don't know what you and the town council were up to or how many people you hurt, and I don't really care. But, if I was you, I would skip town immediately, drive out of New Jersey, and straight through to Key West tonight. I wouldn't even stop to pay tolls along the way." McNamara said.

"So that's it then. Thirty-five years and I get shoved out the door."

'I'm sorry, but you did this to yourself. Whatever you did a long time ago has come back to roost. Don't take anyone else down with you." McNamara said.

"Fine," Browning said, throwing the still full cup of coffee in the trash can as coffee splatter stained the walls above the trash can.

"Where are you going?" McNamara asked.

"I have one final stop to make before leaving town," Browning replied.

"What about your resignation?"

"I'll leave it in the toilet stall after I wipe my ass with it. Feel free to reach in there and grab it." Browning hollered back to him.

October 28, 2022
Saturday 10:45pm

Most of the neighborhood lights were already out. The few which remained on were remnants of those who chose to call Cape May their home during the off-season winter and fall months. The empty houses were reminders of the transitory migration of Cape May's citizens between seasons. Soon Browning would count himself among those migrating, only on a permanent basis. He sat in his personal car, a mid-size low, mileage sedan, which was far more uncomfortable than the Ford explorer police vehicle the department took back earlier this morning after the events of the parade.

The breeze emanating from the ocean shore howled and struck off and over the sedan shaking the vehicle every so often as Browning sat in the silence with the engine off. Dressed in the same black outfit and ski cap he wore when he visited Dr. McDonough, Browning was surveying the street, checking the rearview mirrors, and watching the road against the promenade in front of him for any signs of traffic. The sedan he was parked in sat adjacent to a blue rental house against the backdrop of Mario's pizzeria and the Excalibur hotel. Being the former police chief had its advantages. He knew where all the security cameras were located and their blind spots.

The camera he would need to worry about faced the boardwalk promenade and was situated on top of Mario's pizzeria. The camera captured the entirety of the boardwalk and pavilion leading out onto the beach.

Browning looked behind him and stared at the crowded backseat littered with clothing thrown together out of his closet and shelves. This was not how he intended to pack up to leave town when thoughts of retirement first came into his mind, to be run out by a serial killer and ostracized by his department and the community. The rest of the household items could be sent for, packed up by men who Browning had never met, and driven to Key West. Of course, he could just sell everything at an estate sale and start over fresh. Right now, he just wanted to be on the boat he hadn't bought yet in Key West, drinking his beer and fishing for Marlin. Forgetting about this nightmare.

Instead, there was one more job to finish. Browning would be leaving for Key West after this one last pit stop tonight, and lollygagging at the house while waiting for the Grim Reaper to appear was not on the top of his to-do list. Browning pulled the nine-millimeter sidearm from its holster and rechecked the gun to ensure safety was off and a round was in the chamber. It was the fifth time he had done this check of the nine-millimeter since he began packing his bags, but the checking of the firearm seemed to provide a level of comfort when everything else had already fallen into disarray.

Browning placed the firearm into the pocket of his black North face coat and pulled the matching black ski cap on his head, leaving his face exposed. Reaching into the opposite side pocket, Browning produced the fourteen-inch black Mag-lite, the same one he had beaten McDonough with yesterday. The Mag-lite still worked as Browning clicked the light on and off. It was time to get to the truth and catch up with the past.

Exiting the vehicle, the nighttime wind coming from the beach ahead of him stung his face, and on instinct, Browning balled up his fists for warmth and placed his hands on the inside of his jacket pockets. Careful to stay to the left of the pizzeria and avoid the walkway, Browning climbed up onto the concrete boardwalk. Trudging over the small wooden fence and through the endangered sea grass, sticker bushes, and brush uphill in the sand with the full force of the wind coming from the ocean howling in his face. Walking about fifty yards onto the beach, Browning started to make a right. The camera's located on top of the pizzeria did not have night vision. Anyone reviewing the camera's recordings at a later date would have difficulty spotting him walking along the black background of the ocean along the beach.

Once he cleared the camera's location, he would stop along the beach and check to ensure he wasn't being followed. Sounds were drowned out by crashing waves. The clouds in the sky moved quickly along, allowing light from the partial moon and white specks of stars to peek out before being enveloped and swallowed by the heavens once more. The walk through the sand took longer than he remembered. Maybe he was losing a step or two as he advanced in age.

After ten minutes, Browning stopped at the front of the concrete World War II bunker. The same bunker Browning sat watching from the observatory by the Historic Light House and reminiscing about when the body of Gil Epson was found in the steamer trunk. It almost seemed like fate he should be brought back here once again. Brought back to the place where everything started all those years ago and where this case should end now had a certain symmetry in them.

Removing the fourteen-inch Mag-light from his jacket, Browning pushed the rubber circle in the back and watched the bright stream of light hit a large rectangular piece of ply-wood board, which was full of graffiti tacked onto the entryway of the bunker. Browning placed his free hand along the right side of the covering board, found the notch where his fingers fit in, and put the flashlight back into his jacket. Reaching with both hands into the groove, Browning began pulling on the wooden board.

Placing his leg on the concrete slab and pushing off the board began to pull away from the concrete, and Browning could see the long nails protruding from the board on his side. After several heaving attempts, Browning removed the board from the doorway.

Browning was sucking for air and placed his hands on his knees, trying to catch his breath. He recalled removing that board almost thirty years ago was a much easier task. Standing upright and stretching his back out, Browning reproduced the flashlight and produced a series of keys with his opposite hand.

The keys belonged to the Chief of Police, which granted him access to all the padlocks and restricted areas, including beaches, parks, and historical landmarks throughout Cape May.

McNamara had neglected to have Browning return the township keys in his haste to fire him this morning. Sure, Cape May would ask him to return the Ford Explorer, but a set of keys would be forgotten and overlooked.

The steel door to the concrete bunker was rusted over from the gradual beating of the incoming tide and salt air. One cut from the doorway would result in a complete series of tetanus injections. Reaching up to the top of the door, Browning grabbed the latch secured with a padlock changed every year to avoid corrosion from the elements. The padlock was placed on the upper part of the doorway to prevent damage from the incoming sea levels, which increased yearly, with the bottom portion of the bunker becoming submerged regularly during high tide.

The padlock should have been changed at the end of September. Inserting the key inside the padlock, Browning opened the lock on his first try. Placing the padlock in his pocket, Browning stood still, hearing the continued beating of the ocean on the beach, and took a last look around him. Not seeing anyone following him, he entered the historical bunker.

Upon entering the World War II bunker, two sets of stairs, one going up and to the left and another going right and down, presented themselves. Browning chose to descend on the right and had forgotten about the level of still-sitting murky ocean water that hadn't receded and remained to stagnate below. Without hesitation, Browning pushed forward off the last dry step and wadded thigh deep into the cold dark sea water keeping the flashlight angled up and high to avoid any underwater obstructions.

Clearing the main hallway below and pushing through the foul salt-smelling murk, Browning cleared the food service area of the facility and was working towards the living quarters where the officers had slept over eighty years ago.

The living quarter rooms were placed on both sides of the hallway adjacent to one another. Browning was shining the light from the Mag-light over the top of the room numbers until he found one with stenciling above the door frame; room fifty-seven still inscribed above the doorframe. Placing his shoulder into the half-closed door and following a brief struggle, Browning pushed the door ajar enough to allow him to enter room fifty-seven.

Lumbering to the back of the room to a steel shutter, Browning placed the mini-mag light on the nearest empty decaying rusted bedframe. As the flashlight beam rocked from side to side, Browning grasped onto the deteriorating handle frame of the shutter bar and lifted it. The steel shutters were employed by the bunkers residents to store their personal items while they were stationed in Cape May during the war while looking out for German submarines.

The shutter screeched and plodded as Browning raised the handle frame, positioning his feet in the water while extending his biceps and shoulders to gain leverage as the rusted shutter gave way, going up one notch at a time. In a sudden burst of energy, the remaining shutter jolted up, exposing a giant blue duffel bag sitting in a lone container.

Licking his lips and taking a gulp, Browning reached for the Mag-light stationed on the bed frame to his side and looked over the black stained and mildewed bag. The bag was different than when Browning remembered stowing it here all those years ago. Time had eaten away at the lining and color of the bag, darkening it with mildew and eating away patches into the stretched fabric. As Browning ran the beam of light over the top of the bag where the zipper was, he saw crusted rust embedded into the zipper's notches.

This was close enough to answer any questions or doubts he had, but he was already here and had to know for sure. Taking his hands, Browning reached into two partially torn pieces of fabric from the duffel bag and pulled them apart. The years of wear on the duffel bag made ripping the bag open an easier task. When the tear was complete, Browning shone the light inside the bag and could still see the bones of Jennifer Martin inside. The yellow shirt hung from her remains as her skull and bones stared at Browning. Browning adverted his eyes, covering his mouth as he puked and swallowed it in a gag reflex.

He had to be sure all those years ago; it was another lifetime ago. Jennifer Martin was still deceased, and where Browning left her. Wiping his chin with the back of his hand, Browning was going to return the duffel bag and close the steel shutter when the feeling he was not alone crept up over the back of his neck, like a bug feeling he was about to be stepped on. Browning reached for the holster on his side hip.

"I wouldn't grab that weapon if I were you." The voice from behind him said. It was a voice Browning took less than a second to recognize, McNamara. The temptation and urge to draw from his holster gripped Browning.

"Did you see something you didn't like in there, Clyde?" McNamara asked ribbing him. "Keep your hands up, and don't do anything stupid. I would hate to kill you so close to the end of this adventure."

Sloshing through the water and with a beam of light covering Browning from behind, McNamara came up and placed his firearm into the back of Browning's neck while simultaneously removing Browning's gun from its holster and throwing it into the water behind him.

"Do what I say, and don't make any sudden moves, or I will kill you right here. Place your hands behind your back." McNamara threatened, jamming the pistol into the back of Browning's back.

At a slow pace and with no other options remaining, Browning conceded and placed his arms behind his back, where a pair of handcuffs were placed on him.

"We are going to take a little walk. Follow my instructions." McNamara ordered, jamming his gun into Browning's ribs. "Now move."

October 28, 2022
Saturday 11:22pm

With his hands cuffed behind him, Browning had no way to brace himself when he was shoved face-first into the sand outside the bunker on the beach. Picking his head up from the sand, Browning looked back towards McNamara. The right side of Browning's face glittered with the sandy granules before propping himself up onto his knees. McNamara kept the pistol trained at him from five feet away.

"You had to know it was going to come to this, didn't you?" McNamara asked. "All of your friends picked off methodically. You didn't really think you were going to make it to Key West, did you?"

"Fuck you." Browning snarled, spitting sand from his mouth.

"I appreciate the kind words; please continue to get up and make your way towards the observation deck," McNamara replied.

The beach was illuminated by only the moon and stars, with the waves crashing behind him on the shore as the solitary light rotated from the top of the lighthouse as the beam of light passed overhead. The observation deck separating the bird sanctuary surrounding the Cape May Light House from the beach was still visible in the darkness as McNamara pushed the plodding Browning in the center of the back with the sight of the pistol to make him move.

"You know, I thought you had me figured out pretty early on from the start," McNamara said. "When I walked in on you tearing apart my hotel room. I thought you had me for sure. But you hadn't figured me out. In fact, searching my room and coming up empty crossed me off your list and only made you confide in me a bit more." McNamara continued talking as the two men stood on top of the wooden planks on top of the bird sanctuary and began walking through the Historical Light House parking lot.

"Head for the entrance of the lighthouse," McNamara said.

"I just want to know why go through all this? Why target the council and me? Why the Grim Reaper act?" Browning asked McNamara, keeping his head down to watch where he was walking without the use of his bound arms.

"All of your questions will be answered in time," McNamara answered. "Standing at the gate ahead is one of those answers now."

Browning squinted in the dark and could just see the silhouette of a dark-clad figure pacing the front gate of the lighthouse. The figure became less obscured as Browning traversed the parking lot and came onto the sidewalk. McNamara continued his prodding by poking him in the back with the pistol. Browning approached the dark figure and could see the unmistakable robe and the skull face mask of the Grim Reaper.

"There's no need to wear that silly get-up Jennifer Martin if that's what you want to pretend to call yourself," Browning said. Pulling the hood back, the Grim Reaper placed her hands over her face and pulled the mask off to reveal the pony-tailed blonde woman calling herself Jennifer Martin.

"Her body is in the bunker. Clyde led me straight to her, just like we hoped." McNamara said to her.

"So, it was you I chased through the parade to the parking lot. Makes sense now you had an accomplice; McNamara knew where the cameras were located and could disable them ahead of time to aid in your escape. Where did you end up hiding? How did you get away at the parade? Where did you disappear to?"

"I hid in the trunk of a parked police car. I hit the switch on the key fob, and the trunk popped open. I hopped right in, closing the trunk behind me." Jennifer Martin giggled.

"So, if you are not Jennifer Martin, who are you then?" Browning asked.

"Let me tell you a story as we go for a walk. Head inside the lighthouse and up the stairs, please."

"You beat Doctor McDonough up pretty well. He'll spend at least a few days in the hospital. Knowing I wasn't Jennifer, I can only guess you would have done the same to me or worse before you left for Key West tonight." The woman dressed as the Grim Reaper said, guiding Browning to the steel staircase as McNamara locked the lighthouse door behind him.

"Your turn still might come." Browning retorted.

"Up the stairs, big boy," McNamara said, giving Browning a shove.

Jennifer Martin walked ahead of Browning up the spiral staircase while McNamara followed behind him, keeping the gun trained on his back. "Was McDonough in on your Grim Reaper scheme as well?" Browning asked.

"No. Doctor McDonough was an unwilling accomplice, shall we say." Jennifer Martin said, turning her head to talk to Browning as they proceeded up the lighthouse stairs.

"I grabbed the Doctor's hand when I knew your friend Biaggi from the pizzeria was observing us from the window. We; John and I knew if Biaggi saw us, he would call you, and you would suspect the Doctor of being involved with the Reaper. Telling McDonough, the story about remembering my childhood would make you lead us right to Jennifer Martin's remains. The holding hand act with the Doctor lent credibility to the story I told him about remembering seeing you arrive to visit Linda Martin during the summer."

"How did you know I had an affair with Linda Martin?" Browning asked.

"Because we were there when you came over every day all those years ago. We were nine-year-old's playing in the yard with Jennifer when you would pull up in your police cruiser. We would exit the front yard and go upstairs to the neighbor's second-story window and watch you two exchange intimacies from the window in the next house," The woman pretending to be Jennifer Martin said.

"I was that neighbor, of course. My family rented the house next door to Jennifer's every summer." McNamara said. "The day Jennifer disappeared, we saw you carry her body out of the house wrapped in a blanket from that second-story window out of the back door and place her in your trunk. Of course, no one could have predicted what happened next."

The trio exited the stairwell at the top of the lighthouse, and the revolving light rotating across them bathed them in light for a brief second.

"So, what did happen next?" Browning asked.

The woman pretending to be Jennifer Martin turned towards Browning, struck him in the shoulder, and pressed her thumb down. Browning felt the hypodermic needle stick him as the burning release of fluids entered his bloodstream. Within seconds, the revolving light was overwhelming his field of vision, a haze blurred his sight, and the two people in front of him became four and then six. Browning dropped to his knees before falling to his side as he lost consciousness.

***

Browning's vision was still muddled as McNamara's face came into view as he awoke. The salt air was refreshing, helping him breathe as the fog began to lift from his brain. They were still upstairs on the top floor of the lighthouse but outside the glassed-encased searchlight. "There you are big guy. You'll want to be awake for the big reveal."

McNamara said, gently slapping the cheek of Browning's face.

His head shifted in a circle, and he could see he was no longer handcuffed from behind but instead seated in a chair. A chair with wheels. Despite a grunt of strength, Browning had no power to raise his arms or move his legs to exit the chair.

"Just take it easy. We filled you with enough tranquilizers to ensure you won't get up for the next thirty or forty minutes. Have you guessed who she is yet?" McNamara asked Browning.

"No." Browning gurgled, spit, and drooled as he tried to talk but did not have control of his mouth's functions.

"I'll let her tell it to you. You should hear it from her." McNamara said as the woman dressed as the Grim Reaper stepped forward.

"You can imagine my surprise when I came home from playing one summer day, only to find that you had murdered my father under false pretenses. You planted the evidence of Jennifer Martin's underwear in my father's work van and used that as an excuse to murder him in his ice cream parlor.

"You planted the pistol on him after you gunned him down in cold blood. You became a town hero killing a pedophile, but you were actually covering up your own brutal murder. My father was Evan Peterson, and after his death, I was institutionalized until my aunt and uncle took me in to live with them in Minnesota.

"It wasn't until years later when I found out the Ice Cream Parlor my father owned and should have inherited was stolen by the town council via eminent domain. The property was worth millions of dollars even back then. Of course, Anthony Biaggi, the lead town council member, benefited by having the inside track to purchase the property at a discounted rate. Of course, at that moment, I was able to piece together the town council's involvement in my father's death as extending beyond your limited capabilities Chief.

"Morris Armstrong received his percentage cut of the real estate transaction brokering the sale of the property. Gilbert Epson, who owned the marina, lent Biaggi money to purchase the property at usury rates. Epson admitted before he died, it was Reverend Mulvaney who took a hefty handout yearly in the collection plate from Biaggi to go along with voting to steal the property via eminent domain. You, of course, end up as the hero and ran for election as Chief of Police. While covering up the disappearance of Jennifer Martin.

"All those years I thought I was crazy believing my dad was innocent until I was in college, but then who should I stumble across but Peter Carlson, the neighbor I played with at his summer house when I was growing up in Cape May. Peter remembers me, and we connect in more ways than one. Peter is going to school for Criminal Justice, and our connection to growing up on the Jersey Shore brings us back together, recalling and tracing our memories of Jennifer Martin and my father. During our most intimate conversations, we devise a plan.

Peter changes his name and applies for a new social security number. He becomes John McNamara and joins the Minnesota police department. He applies yearly to be an officer in Cape May and is turned down every time. When it looks like you are about to get away with your crime, detective John McNamara is hired to replace you as the current Chief of Police in Cape May. Ironic how the webs of fate all return home. On your way to hell, I want you to remember my name is Laurie Peterson, and you murdered my father Evan and framed him as a pedophile, you son of a bitch." Laurie Peterson spat.

"It's time," McNamara said, taking a steel chain attached via padlock to the steel railing surrounding the outside of the encased rotating searchlight while taking the opposite end and securing the chain with a second padlock around the drugged Browning's neck.

Laurie Peterson reached toward the floor and picked up an item. Browning's vision sparked when he recognized the object Laurie Peterson had in her possession; the rotating searchlight passed over her and illuminated a small red container of gasoline.

Unscrewing the cap of the gas container, Laurie began pouring the gasoline on top of Browning's head. Despite squeezing his eyes closed, the liquid burned in his eyes and tasted foul in his mouth. When the last of the gasoline was poured on top of Browning, Laurie took Browning's hands and placed them on the empty gasoline container and around the handle and cap. Making sure to put Browning's fingerprints on the evidence.

"Your legacy in this town is finished. Tomorrow after they find your badly charred body hung from the top of this Lighthouse, a search of your house will be conducted. A suicide note will be typed on your computer admitting your involvement in the killing of the council so you could remain on as Chief of Police as long as the investigation was ongoing. It will be signed by you with your fingerprints on the paper." Laurie Peterson said.

"Do you have any last words for us before meeting the devil?" McNamara asked.

"Ack wasss int me. Leeendar sk Leeendar. Puease, dunot bun me." Browning pled, squinting his eyes from the gasoline, and fumbling his words through the sedative. Browning raised his head slightly as he tried to form coherent words.

"Did you understand what he just said?" McNamara asked, leaning towards the immobile Browning, and turning to Laurie.

"No. I didn't catch it. Guess it doesn't much matter anyway." Laurie said, kicking the wheelchair Browning was sitting on back. The push from Laurie's kick sent the wheelchair reeling backward and off the vacant space of the lighthouse where there was no safety railing.

The duo stood next to each other, looking at the expression on Browning's face that remained stagnant as he was pushed from the top of the lighthouse. As the wheelchair dipped off the side of the lighthouse, the chain attached to the railing ran rapidly, pulling until jerking in a final movement. Hanging Browning by the neck. Laurie took the matchbook, lit the gasoline-soaked chain, and watched the flame dance over the ledge of the lighthouse.

The pair moved close to the ledge and watched the fiery swinging pendulum of Clyde Browning hanging from the top of the Cape May Lighthouse as the wheelchair fell to the earth below.

November 6th, 2022
Tuesday 7:21am

Linda Martin returned from her early morning run to her house and up the stairs to her porch. The November chill paired with the grey morning sky as the bright red sun began peeking through the clouds in a futile attempt to warm the night's thaw on the rocks in her yard. Reaching under her door mat and pulling the carpet aside, Linda produced the key hidden under the mat. The doorknob turned and the door opened before she could insert the key.

She must have forgotten to lock the door on her way out for her run. It wouldn't be the first time her age and memory had begun to slip. For years she had started to forget where she had placed items around the house or common words she used regularly. The memory loss was a side effect of old age, but this repetitive act of locking the door every morning before her run was built into her routine. It was unnatural to forget to lock the door as she placed the key back under the mat and went inside.

The house was the usual empty as she walked through her living room. Locking the door behind her, Linda kicked her shoes off and checked her Fitbit watch to see the morning's mileage. Over four miles were logged, and the day was just beginning. Into the kitchen, she opened the refrigerator and pulled water from the bottom door shelf, unscrewing the cap. Linda took a swig before placing the lid back on the bottle. Next was the morning shower and food shopping, she thought as she walked back through the living room and stopped midway.

Sitting on the couch holding a giant scythe was a person dressed in a large black hooded cloak, and when Linda's eyes met this person on the sofa, the black-cloaked head raised up to reveal the skull and empty eyes of the Grim Reaper sitting in her living room. Linda's heart sank. Her first instinct was surprise, a startled leap as she clutched her chest in instinct. She thought of running, the locked door fifteen feet from her, but the Grim Reaper was sitting on the couch closer to the door than she was.

Her sight turned to the oversized mildew and ripped, faded blue canvas bag on the floor, and her heart sank in her chest. Without needing confirmation, Linda already knew what was inside the torn duffel bag at the Grim Reaper's feet.

"What do you want?" Linda asked the Grim Reaper choking her way through the short sentence.

"You know what we want." A voice replied from the bedroom. John McNamara appeared, walking out of the bedroom holding a gun.

"May I have a seat then?" Linda asked.

"Of course," McNamara said, waving his arm for her to pick a seat. Linda chose the chair opposite the Grim Reaper in front of the large blue canvas bag.

"Is she in there? Is Jennifer in the bag?" Linda asked, and the Grim Reaper nodded in ascent.

"I knew the moment I met you were not my daughter. You had everyone else fooled. Even Clyde, on some level, wanted Jennifer to somehow be alive. But not me. I guess it was always going to come down to this. The past was always going to catch up with me. You can take the ridiculous outfit off now. I'll go quietly." Linda said with tears streaming down her face.

The Grim Reaper removed the mask, and Laurie Peterson sat face to face with Linda.

"I thought you might be finished after you framed Clyde for the Reaper murders, but I guess it makes sense you would finish everyone involved for Jennifer's disappearance," Linda said.

"Actually, we didn't figure it out until Browning said his last words. While he begged for us not to burn him. He said he was innocent and to ask you." McNamara said, standing behind her.

"Poor Clyde, he loved me and would have done anything for me. Of course, seeing you sitting here in my living room and seeing my daughter's remains, I can only suppose you are Evan Peterson's daughter. I am sorry about what they did to you and your father. He was a good man. I didn't think about him or what the town council did to you both for many years. I was so caught up in my own grief." Linda said.

"We want to know why you protected the man who murdered your daughter Ms. Martin?" McNamara asked.

"Is that what you think? That I was protecting Clyde? It was the other way around. On the day she died, Clyde and I were upstairs in the bedroom, fooling around, when Jennifer burst in to confront us. Clyde was getting dressed, and I was upset. Jennifer went on and on about telling her father about our affair and how I was an 'unfaithful whore'. She kept repeating those words, calling me an 'unfaithful whore.'

"The accusations were cutting my thin skin like a knife. Jennifer was right, of course, about my infidelity, but despite my passion for Clyde, I still wanted to be married and a mother on some level. As we argued, Jennifer threatened to tell her father about our affair. I took my hand and slapped Jennifer across the face. I don't even remember slapping her that hard, but I hit her. Her head bounced off the corner of the makeup desk. I heard her neck snap as she went limp on the floor.

"I put my hand to my mouth and froze, repeating her name under my breath. I was in shock. Clyde rushed over and began CPR, but I knew she was dead even then. Gone forever. Her last words to me 'unfaithful whore.' Forever stuck in my ears. Clyde wanted to call the police, to call an ambulance. It was an accident, after all. I cried. I would be sent to jail for killing my own daughter. Clyde took pity on me in his own way. He loved me even then and, at that moment, would do anything. Clyde wrapped her in the bedroom blanket and took her out the back door. I never asked what he did with her body.

"For years, I self-medicated, sleeping days then weeks away. Refusing to see Clyde or even speak to my own husband. Then one day, I got up and started pulling my life together. I divorced my husband and started running. I never saw Clyde intimately again. I have never been with another man since the day Jennifer died.

Despite Clyde's repeated attempts to reconnect with me, I rebuked him at every turn. I never wanted to be reminded of that day again, but it has never left me. Her death is always here in my every thought, every day, every night. Part of me wanted you to be Jennifer, just like her father believes you are. But I knew you weren't."

"You know what has to happen next, don't you?" McNamara asked, still standing behind her.

"Yes. I only ask you to find a final resting place for my daughter. She deserves that. Years of being locked away somewhere without being afforded a final chance for peace. The dignity of being properly buried. You can do that, can't you?" The tears started again from Linda's eyes.

"I promise," McNamara said.

Linda filled the bathtub with warm water and removed all her clothes except her panties and bra. Slipping into the warm bath as the water ran, Laurie Peterson took her seat on the toilet bowl after closing the lid and held Linda's hand for a brief moment. "I'm ready," Linda said, nodding her head.

Laurie removed a box cutter from underneath her cloak and handed it to Linda.

"Thank you for bringing my daughter home to me. I hope you can find peace." Linda said before pushing up the black slide knob as the metal blade protracted from the yellow plastic. Placing the knife in her forearm, she grimaced in pain as she made a vertical cut against the arteries in her left hand.

Before the tingling sensation rendered her left hand motionless, Linda placed the box cutter in her left hand and cut from her wrist up to her forearm. Both cuts ran deep as the blood mixed into the warm tub of water.

The blade fell from her hand and into the red water. Placing her head back on the porcelain tub, Linda kept her eyes trained on the woman dressed as the Grim Reaper who had put the skeleton mask back over her face as they watched each until Linda slipped away and closed her eyes, sleeping for eternity.

August 5, 2023

Monday 10:24am

The older woman with the badly dyed red hair and matching red spectacles barely raised her head as the thin man in the grey suit approached her desk.

"Excuse me, Mrs. Stewart." The thin man said, reading the plaque on the desk.

Raising her head from the litany of paperwork sprawled on her desk, she pushed the rim of her glasses up on her face to get a better look at the thin man standing before her. Dressed in a dark grey suit with a mixed match yellow and black striped tie. His hair was thinning on top of his head, and his face was gaunt and pale.

She ascertained the gentleman before her was not a local resident of Cape May but rather someone who did not get out much. Judging by the lack of color on his face and the cheap suit, he was probably an attorney.

"Can I help you, sir?" Carrie Stewart asked.

The man pulled his credentials from his jacket pocket and flipped them open. The picture was too far away to get a positive identification, but the bright blue lettering was unmistakable. F.B.I.

"I'm Special Agent Wyatt Tennant. Federal Bureau of Investigation. I was hoping to speak to the Chief of Police." Officer Tennant said, closing his credentials.

"Do you have an appointment?" Carrie asked.

"No, I was passing through on a separate case, and after months of playing phone, tag decided to take a chance and stop in. I hope it's not too much of an inconvenience."

"What's this in reference to, sir?" Carrie Stewart asked.

"It's about the Grim Reaper murders from last year," Wyatt replied.

"One second. I'll see if Chief McNamara is available." Carrie said, picking up her telephone and pushing a button before covering her mouth and speaking into the receiver just low enough so Agent Tennant could not hear her voice. When she was finished speaking, she hung up the phone and placed the receiver down.

"You are in luck. The Chief has a few minutes to spare to speak with you. He's in with his new wife. Lucky for you, he just returned from his honeymoon yesterday. If you showed you up any earlier than today, you might have missed him. He's through that door on your left. Just knock before you go in." Carrie Stewart instructed, pointing to the door.

Agent Wyatt Tennant approached the door and knocked as instructed by the secretary and heard a voice say to come in from behind the door. Walking through the doorway, Wyatt was met halfway inside by Chief John McNamara, his wife, a blonde was sitting on top of his desk.

"Chief John McNamara." McNamara said introducing himself. Getting up and shaking Agent Tennant's hand, Chief John McNamara towered over the skinny, balding FBI agent in physical size.

"This is my wife, Jennifer McNamara. I wasn't expecting any visitors this morning. We just returned from our honeymoon, so please excuse the informality of this meeting." McNamara said as Jennifer waved while remaining seated on the corner of the desk.

"Is there a chance I could speak to you privately?" Agent Tennant asked, looking away from Jennifer.

"Anything you can say to me, you can say in front of my wife. I don't hold secrets from her. So please sit. Can I offer you some coffee or water?"

McNamara asked, resuming his seat behind the desk while Jennifer continued sitting on the corner.

"No, thank you. I just had breakfast at Uncle Bill's Pancake House a few minutes ago." Agent Tennant replied.

"You are here about the Grim Reaper Murders and the former Chief of Police Clyde Browning. I thought we sent your office everything last year?" McNamara asked.

"You did send over the files, but I had just a few questions. My specialty with the Bureau is abnormal psychology, specifically serial killers, and their psychology. I assist in putting together a dossier of their background and look for indicative patterns into what motivated them." Agent Tennant said.

"I follow you so far. What can I help you with?" McNamara asked.

"Well, asking around, I understand you shadowed Chief Browning for the days before his death and during the Grim Reaper investigation." Agent Tennant asked.

"That's correct. While Browning prepared for his upcoming retirement, I was learning on the job." McNamara replied.

"That's a subject I wanted to speak with you about. You mentioned Chief Browning's pending retirement. Did he speak about retirement regularly, was he looking forward to his retirement, or was he upset about his retirement? I'm trying to gain some insight into the type of man Chief Browning was."

"I would say he was in denial about his retirement. He hadn't even started packing this office up. He was still working and had his hands in the day-to-day operations until he was relieved of duty." McNamara answered.

"But if I'm not mistaken, on the night he committed suicide on top of the Cape May Lighthouse, his car was found parked a few blocks away near the boardwalk loaded with suitcases and gym bags containing his clothes and some personal items. If he wasn't planning on leaving, why pack everything up into the back of his car?" Agent Tennant asked.

"I'm afraid that's beyond my role as Chief of Police to speculate about what is going on inside the mind of a murderer Agent Tennant," McNamara replied.

"Exactly right. Let's talk about the mind of the murderer. In this case, you have a man, a law-abiding man who, as far as we know, had no history of killing people or breaking any laws for almost sixty years. Then all of a sudden, he snaps and creates a persona with which he kills several well-known associates, including his friend Anthony Biaggi. It doesn't make any sense." Agent Tennant said.

"If you ask me, he was paranoid. There are several statements from the Officer's involved in this case, particularly the Cape May Sheriff's Office, about his propensity to want to control the investigation. I believe he lost control of his life when he lost the town's confidence as Chief, and I was slated to take his place. The suicide note found in his home printed on his computer indicated as much." McNamara said.

"I'm glad you brought that up. If, as you say, Chief Browning despised losing his office, why not go after the current town council responsible for ousting him. In fact, why not take it out on the man set to replace him. You. Why not come after you? As the Grim Reaper, he would have been absolved of any wrongdoing and potentially allowed to continue as Chief of Police until another replacement was selected." Agent Tennant speculated.

"Do you really think he may have considered murdering me? I had never considered that a possibility until now." McNamara said, turning to his wife, feigning concern.

"Thank goodness he didn't come after you," Jennifer said, placing her hand on her chest. "You saw what that brute did to poor Dr. McDonough."

"Another question. During the inventory of Browning's personal effects, a set of keys and a padlock were found inside his jacket pocket. Did your office ever find out what these keys or the padlock belonged to? I checked the keys with the padlocks used to secure the chain around his neck and to the railing on top of the lighthouse, but none of the keys would work to open them. Were any keys to those padlocks ever recovered?"

"No, the padlock had to be sawed off so the chain could be removed from his charred remains. Regarding the padlock in his jacket pocket, I think we all assumed it was another set he brought with him." McNamara replied.

"One last thing, off the record." Agent Tennant said.

"Of course." Chief McNamara said, nodding his head in assent.

"Are you satisfied with the outcome of the investigation?" Agent Tennant asked.

"It is the official position of the Cape May County Police Department and my opinion that Chief Browning was the Grim Reaper killer. His suicide note and the fact the murders ceased following his death offer conclusive evidence of this. Also, he was the first on the scene during several of the murders and offered no alibi's for any of the time these murders were committed." Chief McNamara said.

"What about an accomplice? According to your report, when Anthony Biaggi was discovered inside the metal bull cauldron, you subdued the parade float driver, and another suspect eluded Chief Browning." Agent Tennant asked.

"I've thought a lot about the day of the parade. It was the driver's statement he was hired anonymously via a personal advertisement. I suspect Chief Browning hired the person pretending to be the Grim Reaper and deliberately let them escape.

All the security cameras in the parking lot were disabled, again indicating to the Police Department someone with insider knowledge of where those cameras were placed. So, anticipating the actor's escape during the parade, Browning disabled the cameras ahead of time." Chief McNamara suggested.

"And the person hired to be the Grim Reaper that day, what of him?" Agent Tennant asked.

"Gone with the wind. Realizing the mistake they made in accepting the job, that person disappeared." Chief McNamara said.

"That's some heavy conjecture. It is, therefore, possible the Grim Reaper got away on the day of the parade and that Browning was subsequently murdered and then framed." Agent Tennant said.

"I don't believe so. Again, the position of the Cape May Police Department is the case is closed and that Chief Browning was the Grim Reaper. Unless you have any evidence to the contrary." Chief McNamara said.

"No, I don't have evidence to the contrary. Thank you for the interview. I may hang around Cape May and do some independent research and interviews for the file. Congratulations again on your wedding." Agent Tennant said, closing his notepad and standing up.

Chief McNamara stood up also and shook Agent Tennant's hand from across the desk. "If you need anything else regarding this investigation, please let my office know, and we will be more than happy to assist."

Heading for the office door, Tennant stopped and turned toward Jennifer, still sitting on the desk. "How long did you two know each other before deciding to get married?"

"A little over a year. We actually met during the Grim Reaper murders investigation. Sometimes it seems like we have known each other since childhood, though." Jennifer said, smiling.

Tennant nodded his head and exchanged smiles. "Well, congratulations again." He said before exiting the office and closing the door behind him.

Resuming his seat beside his new bride, McNamara rubbed her leg.

"He knows Clyde Browning isn't the Grim Reaper. We should get ahead of this." Jennifer Martin said.

"Don't do anything reckless. He doesn't have anything. He's asking questions no one has the answers to. We are safe. Eliminating him would only draw the ire of every Law Enforcement Agency down here. It's best to forget the whole episode and begin our new life together as husband and wife, with our new baby on the way." McNamara said, rubbing her belly.

"You aren't worried then?" Jennifer asked taking his hand in hers on top of her pregnant stomach.

"No. The Grim Reaper murders are in the past. Clyde Browning and his role in murdering the former town council will live on in documentaries, books, and podcasts for years. You better get used to people running around asking questions. But in the end, that's all it will ever add up to is questions and theories coming from crackpots and you tube experts.

"People love a good ending, and right now Clyde Browning is the knot on the bow of a perfectly good ending. The perfect patsy. The Grim Reaper murders will forever add to the lore and mystery of Cape May's history long after we are gone and forgotten." McNamara said before kissing his wife.

AUTHOR'S NOTE

Thank you for reading The Cape May Murders. Please follow me and sign up for my free newsletter at **Christophermichaelblake.com**. Many of the places detailed in this work are real places, so please visit them if you visit Cape May. Unfortunately, though there is no actual Biaggi's currently in Cape May, New Jersey. However, the Nor'easter referenced as occurring in 1962 is a real event that devasted Cape May.

In researching this novella, I referred to Jospeh G. Burcher & Robert Kenselaar's book Remembering South Cape May: The Jersey Shore town that vanished into the sea and Joe J. Jordan's illustrated book Cape May Point: The Illustrated History: 1875 to Present. Both books do an excellent job of detailing the history of Cape May and come highly recommended.

If you enjoyed reading the Cape May Murders and want to share your experience, please leave a review on Amazon or on Good Reads as this helps indie authors find an audience.

Made in the USA
Middletown, DE
07 June 2023

31864094R10109